CW00860271

CASE FILES

UNS LVED

Sleuthing Adventures

Edited By Allie Jones

First published in Great Britain in 2021 by:

Young Writers
Remus House
Coltsfoot Drive
Peterborough
PE2 9BF
Telephone: 01733 890066
Website: www.youngwriters.co.uk

Printed and bound in the UK by BookPrintingUK
Website: www.bookprintinguk.com
YB0479S

FOREWORD

As long as there have been people, there has been crime, and as long as there have been people, there have also been stories. Crime fiction has a long history and remains a consistent best-seller to this day. It was for this reason that we decided to delve into the murky underworld of criminals and their misdeeds for our newest writing competition.

We challenged secondary school students to craft a story in just 100 words on the theme of 'Unsolved'. They were encouraged to consider all elements of crime and mystery stories: the crime itself, the victim, the suspect, the investigators, the judge and jury. The result is a variety of styles and narrations, from the smallest misdemeanors to the most heinous of crimes. Will the victims get justice or will the suspects get away with murder? There's only one way to find out!

Here at Young Writers it's our aim to inspire the next generation and instill in them a love of creative writing, and what better way than to see their work in print? The imagination and flair on show in these stories is proof that we might just be achieving that aim! The characters within these pages may have to prove their innocence, but these authors have already proved their skill at writing!

CONTENTS

The George Eliot School, Caldwell

Ryan Sarson (13)   1
Sofia Delbusso (14)   2
Nikita Hughes (14)   3
Isobel Harcourt (12)   4
India Adams (14)   5
Jack Kitson (12)   6
Sarah Sharples (13)   7
Ryan Lenton (12)   8
Che Barry (12)   9
Amy Pryke (11)   10
Jacob Marsden (12)   11
Emmie Crook (12)   12
Marcy Ireland-Buck (12)   13
Libby Sayer (12)   14
Emma Thompson-Hamilton (12)   15
Mia Flavel (13)   16
Lily Thompson (14)   17
Jess Mugglestone (14)   18
Amelie Atkinson (12)   19
Thomas Elder (12)   20
Isabelle Cunningham (12)   21
Charlotte Hiscock (12)   22
Nicole Moseley (12)   23
Hollie Wonzeri (13)   24
Joe Ballard (12)   25
James Santos (14)   26
Kelsi Brennan (12)   27
Shelby Tonks (13)   28
Isabel Gudgeon (13)   29
Owen Stokes (11)   30
Milah Ehsan   31
Jacob Hardy (12)   32
Hollie Lister Farrington (12)   33
Lilli Langton (12)   34

Lucy Gibson (14)   35
Harper Ward (12)   36
Lauren Jukes (13)   37
Cerys Attwood (11)   38
Gemma Collins (12)   39
Ava Ellis (12)   40
Lexie Cooper (11)   41
Mollie Haynes (12)   42
Rhys Jones (11)   43
Amy-Leigh Wilson (13)   44
Emma Hemming (11)   45
Dylan Holmes (12)   46
Marissa Lee (11)   47
Marshall Glasspool (13)   48
Erin Spacey (12)   49
Bella Sweeney (11)   50
Chloe Sharrock-White (13)   51
Aimee Morrissey (13)   52

The Hemel Hempstead School, Hemel Hempstead

Hannah Mills (12)   53
Elvin Fedakar (13)   54
Hollie Smith (12)   55
Amy Warren (12)   56
Emily Simpson (13)   57
Rory Barber (12)   58
Aaron Tapimene (13)   59
Alexis Armson (12)   60
Flori Hudson (12)   61
Ella Tremayne   62
Ramone Hibbert (13)   63
Emma Lewis (13)   64
Thomas Twine (13)   65
Anja Mudrinic (13)   66

Alfie Hedges (12)	67	Leila Gilliatt (12)	102
Martha Morris (11)	68	Edward Byrne (13)	103
Seb White (13)	69	Claudia Kelly (12)	104
Archie Hendery (13)	70	Amelia Targett (12)	105
Holly Jewell (13)	71	Jack Newby (12)	106
		Melissa Plater (13)	107

The Purbeck School, Wareham

Isabel Randall (12)	72
Annabelle Jakubas (12)	73
William Douglas (12)	74
Benjamin Sharp (12)	75
Faith Welch (12)	76

The Wren School, Reading

Brandon Davies (14)	77
Iryna Suichymez (12)	78

Tollbar Academy, New Waltham

Maryam Kazemi (13)	79
Esmeralda Kokina (12)	80
Jacob Braithwaite (12)	81
Evie Jacobs (13)	82
Layla Salameh (13)	83
Willow Vickers (13)	84
Esmé Kent (11)	85
Amelia Sharp (13)	86
Felicity Green (13)	87
Chloe Jackson (11)	88
Jared Brewin (12)	89
Faith Swanson (12)	90
Matilda Cuthbert (12)	91
Eva Summers (11)	92
Anisa Safa (11)	93
Grace Grigg (13)	94
Alex Reed (11)	95
Chloe Whitton (13)	96
Jack Walton (12)	97
Hannah Collins (11)	98
Evie Newton (13)	99
Alfie Wood	100
Alexander Hanks (13)	101

Hannah Howden (12)	108
Eden Castle (11)	109
Sophie Clarke (12)	110
Harry Edwards (13)	111
Nathan Gibbs (12)	112
Alfie Winter (13)	113
Lucas Tuplin (11)	114
Dylan Westerby (13)	115
Luke Johnson (11)	116
Joshua Corken (12)	117
Julia Gussmann (12)	118
Nuala Stephenson (12)	119
Harvey Jensen (13)	120
Oliwia Tyczynska (13)	121
Holly Clifford (12)	122
Alisia Smith (14)	123
Lexi-Jo Penney (11)	124
Oscar Gibbon (13)	125
Ryan Howie (13)	126
Lilly Melbourne (12)	127
Matthew Watson (13)	128

Trinity Academy Grammar, Sowerby Bridge

Sophie Calder (13)	129
Erin Lillia Conway (13)	130
Imogen Taylor (13)	131
Adiba Islam (12)	132
Shrena Ramakrishnan (12)	133
Phoebe Graham (13)	134
Eleanor Baines (13)	135
Amelia Czapiewska (13)	136
Lily Roberts (13)	137
Annabel Walker (13)	138
Elena Mirgova (13)	139
Mehek Ali (13)	140
Aliya Rahman (12)	141

Hannaan Arbab (13)   142

Twynham School, Christchurch

Jonathan Purse (12)   143
Maria Butt   144
Ollie Dashwood   145
Mya Lonnen (12)   146
Dylan Winter (12)   147
Isla Crum   148
Claudia Spencer (12)   149
Sophie Nicholson (12)   150
Phoebe Bennett (12)   151
Poppy Miller   152
Ryley Deacon (12)   153
Samuel Hooks (11)   154
Lucas Hayward (12)   155
Molly Kuhne (12)   156
Beth Stewart (12)   157
Chloe Robinson   158
Kitty Johnston (12)   159
Bethany Edwards   160
Aleisha Hughes   161
Leah-Louise Thorn   162
Otto Williams (12)   163
Samuel Chapman (12)   164

Values Academy, Stockingford

Wyatt Mainwaring (14)   165
Kaidon (14)   166
Cameron Fish (15)   167
Camron Milburn (14)   168
Cameron B   169
Elliot Prince (14)   170
Jack Goodman   171
Harvey   172
Curtis Lee   173

Voyage Learning Campus, Worle

Gracelyn Ellis (13)   174
Annabelle A   175
Summer Ellis (12)   176

Logan Smith (13)   177
Fuschia Vass   178

West Hatch High School, Chigwell

Joshua Ssempiira (13)   179
Meghana Pirabaharan (12)   180
Amelie Lo Giudice (12)   181
Lucas Watts (12)   182

Woodcote High School, Coulsdon

Eve Clowes (14)   183
Leo Keene (12)   184
Emma Barron (13)   185
Zach Parker (13)   186
Honey Chard-Latouche (13)   187
Aliyah Khan   188
Kiera Fricker   189
Aidan Leamy (13)   190
Eleanor Robson (14)   191
Jiya Vadher (13)   192
Austen Barnhurst   193
Rebecca Kendall   194
Sydney Holdsworth (11)   195
Toby Ward (12)   196
Lauren Curtis (12)   197
Abigail Hendle   198
Jamie Rouse (12)   199
Zachary Dallman (12)   200
Veisa Zace   201

XP East, Doncaster

Thea Clarkson (14)   202
Ava Fletcher-Bedford (14)   203
Lewis Floyd (13)   204
Sami Fourie (13)   205
Marcus Hague (14)   206
Florence Roberts (14)   207
Ruby Underwood (13)   208
Lucie-Mae Cordell (13)   209
Zak M-Hall (14)   210

THE STORIES

1 LEFT OUT OF 35

The supernatural, not real, so I thought.

It was early morning, an icy-cold breeze came through the open window. My dad read in the newspaper about a disappearing body, suspected grave robber he said.

I arrived at Downhall Elementary, 9am. I sat down in English class, only 18 out of 35 here, bit odd. Miss screamed, "Everyone stay down, stay quiet." Another drill? The alarm rang, children screamed for help. The lights went off and it all went mysteriously silent.

No, it wasn't a grave robber, 'It' was alive and it whispered, "You're the only one left out of 35..."

Ryan Sarson (13)
The George Eliot School, Caldwell

UNKNOWN TRUTH

"Guilty!"
I believe that's incorrect. After examining the shattered remains left beneath the glass window, the fingerprints from the frame couldn't be mine. My alibi has failed to convince them. Their every accusation lingers around my name.
The case has continued despite any danger; the search group introduced a new detective. Immediately, his eyes shot in my direction. I stood stationed like a statue as a tear escaped, dripping down my white face.
A lie detector test is due for all remaining suspects. Would I have to come clean? It's only a matter of time before the truth is released.

Sofia Delbusso (14)
The George Eliot School, Caldwell

DEADPOOL

I had an alibi. I saw him on Thursday night, he left with them, last I ever saw him. Everyone thinks I have something to do with it, I'm quite a mysterious person, quiet too. Sam Jackson's the name. Nothing too wild, fits me really. Nobody cared about me until recently.

"You hacked into a Deadpool didn't you?" The officer had a frustrated tone in his voice.

"No! Of course not! I didn't even know they existed!"

This is the fifth time I've been interrogated.

"Yes, of course!" The policeman folded his arms, sarcastically.

I don't own a laptop... Anymore.

Nikita Hughes (14)
The George Eliot School, Caldwell

UNDER THE STAIRS

I'm Gabriella Montany. I'm a detective working for the 'CA' (it's kind of like the FBI but more secret). I'm on a case of the disappearance of Lady Rose, the daughter of one of the most substantial men in Evergreen.

One day, we found evidence tracking to a house on Peggy Lane, house number 27. We went straight there. When we arrived - around 11am - we strode towards the house and knocked on the door. A fragile woman opened the door, the crew said, "This is obviously the wrong house, it's pointless." Until I noticed a hidden door under the stairs...

Isobel Harcourt (12)
The George Eliot School, Caldwell

TRUTH HURTS, BUT THIS LIE KILLED HIM

"Guilty!" shouted the judge at who everyone thought was the suspect but in actual fact I was. I'd framed an innocent bystander or witness.

I had placed the knife and hammer in his bag. When police arrived they did a bag search of everyone. They found evidence in Orion's computer bag.

"Ash... Ash..." is all I heard when I zoned back in. My lawyer spun round in circles exclaiming, "We won!" over and over again. I felt so bad as the person I framed was my best friend. I betrayed the most supportive person ever. I'm so sorry Orion...

India Adams (14)

The George Eliot School, Caldwell

FOOTBALL FREAK-OUT

Let me set the scene... The year is 1966 and England have just won the World Cup. The streets of London, therefore, are a sea of people cheering and chanting, the perfect place for something to break out... and it did... but abnormally. James was just your ordinary 10-year-old boy, interested in anything that was going on around him so, when people started parading the streets, he obviously joined in. Whilst partying, a hooded man approached him and mouthed, "Take it," handing James a mysterious object. As he took it, the man disappeared, or so he thought...

Jack Kitson (12)
The George Eliot School, Caldwell

THE DEAD OF NIGHT

Working at a cemetery is hard. I don't know why I did this to begin with. I can't lie, many things have happened; people wandering around, ominous noises but I just thought nothing of it until that night...

Working as normal, I came across empty coffins staring back at me. Yet again the strange noises found me. Turning around shakily, eight figures lurked towards me. As they stepped closer, I noticed their bloodshot eyes, rotten skin which had blood cascading from their lifeless bodies, and their deformed faces. That was the last thing I saw that night.

Sarah Sharples (13)
The George Eliot School, Caldwell

WHO'S THERE?

It's December 23rd, it's a cold evening and you wake up to a loud bang. As you walk cautiously down the stairs pans and plates crash against each other like wind chimes. Loud noises that seem untranslatable come from the kitchen, in a deep voice you hear, "Run!" You grab the nearest phone and call 999.

"Hello, what service do you need?" they say, it's followed by a fuzz and the phone hangs up. The power's out. You try to climb out of the window but it's jammed shut, slowly you walk down the stairs and into the cold kitchen...

Ryan Lenton (12)
The George Eliot School, Caldwell

THE FOREST

Have you heard about the dark and eerie forest? The one behind the Millers' House? The forest where the branches creak at night like little children screaming? The forest where the wind whistles through the leaves like ghosts crying from their graves? The forest that looks so tranquil in the sunlight yet so sinister in the night sky? The Miller family has told local children spine-chilling stories about that forest for years. I don't believe the stories they tell, but I won't wander in there on my own, not even in the daylight, just in case. Would you go in?

Che Barry (12)
The George Eliot School, Caldwell

UNSOLVED ROBBERIES

One night, a robbery happened at my house, it was horrific, the robbers left the house empty, everything had been stolen. It then happened another night, then again and again. It was up to the detectives to find and stop the thieves by solving clues. They were very hard to find since they were very sneaky and didn't leave anything behind. The whole detective crew couldn't find any clues at all. Another night passed, it happened again and nobody could find a single clue. Nothing could stop them as they kept robbing houses leaving people to sleep on the floor.

Amy Pryke (11)
The George Eliot School, Caldwell

THE CHOCOLATE CAKE MYSTERY

Mum left the chocolate cake in the middle of the table, giving strict instructions to everyone in the house not to touch it. Thinking it would be safe, she hurried upstairs to get changed before the party. Imagine her surprise (more like uncontrollable rage) when she returned to where the cake should have been, only to find a handful of brown crumbs left on the plate. The finger of suspicion pointed at the three household suspects: the husband, clutching his stomach; the son wiping his mouth and the family dog licking his lips. Which of the three demolished the cake?

Jacob Marsden (12)
The George Eliot School, Caldwell

THE EMPTY GRAVE

Where is he?
As I kept looking around the graveyard, an empty grave
appeared. Me and the other detective looked at each other
with shock, we both looked at the gravestone, it was the
body we were looking for, fear filled our minds! We ran into
the forest nearby.
"The grave looks like it's been empty for a long time," we
said.
As we walked through the forest there was a clue... Fresh
footprints in the squelchy mud. We followed the footprints,
they came to an end, we turned around and behind us was
the body we were looking for...

Emmie Crook (12)
The George Eliot School, Caldwell

THE MURDER OF DETECTIVE SHELLEY

Pacing back and forth around the lab, my head filled with thoughts. There was only one thing I had to do. I couldn't think of anything else. I ran out of the lab, not closing the door, and ran to the graveyard. It was just minutes away. I didn't stop running. I wanted to prove something, although I didn't know what. Inconspicuously, I peered through the gates of the gothic graveyard. I ran to the grave, careless about the dead bodies beneath me. I was shocked. The gravestone read 'Detective Shelley.' That's when I realised, I was the victim.

Marcy Ireland-Buck (12)
The George Eliot School, Caldwell

THE CLOSET

Three trembling bodies. What had they just seen?

Years ago, there were four happy siblings. On the 30th September, around 17:30, the oldest sibling, Thomas, disappeared. No one thought anything of it because this had happened before, he would often go for a walk. Later, it now being around 21:20, still not home, the family started to worry as his curfew was 20:30.

Five years later, no sight of Thomas. The family never went in his closet, so they never expected to find this... but there was Thomas' body hung on a rope. Did he commit suicide?

Libby Sayer (12)
The George Eliot School, Caldwell

GUILTY! UNTIL PROVEN INNOCENT...

Dear Diary,

Today I had an extreme court case. An 11-year-old girl has been accused of robbing a store worker. I could not believe the words that came out of my boss' mouth this morning. I went to court, the suspect was not there. I was really confused (I was there to defend her), then the judge came up to me and said, "Do you know where the suspect is?"
I said, "No."
We looked all around the building for her. The judge went outside and saw her, "Found her!" She was running fast, but we couldn't catch her...

Emma Thompson-Hamilton (12)
The George Eliot School, Caldwell

THE DAY I FOUND HER

Darkness took over my room. At this point in time I didn't know if I would ever find her. No evidence, nothing, I can hear her voice in my head, it's haunting me as if it's my fault she's gone missing. I feel the need that I must look for evidence starting at her favourite coffee shop. On my way I pass the graveyard, only to see a mysterious figure lurking in the shadows. This figure looks familiar, I decide to investigate only to find out it is her, my friend who is missing. She's whispering, "She's here..."

Mia Flavel (13)
The George Eliot School, Caldwell

I KNOW THE TRUTH

"Guilty!"

The judge's word echoed over the courtroom. The room went completely silent as his head fell into his hands. Falsely charged. Now he was going to waste away in jail. I know who did it. A man who was able to get away without being questioned as he seemed completely innocent. I want to bring justice. I need to.

I saw how it happened, he wanted a promotion so she had to die. He planned it out so he'd never be even thought to be the murderer. He succeeded.

They say the dead can't talk, but I will.

Somehow.

Lily Thompson (14)
The George Eliot School, Caldwell

THE VOICE OF MURDER

People think the dead can't talk but ever since I murdered Jacob Walker on August 15th his voice haunts me...
Standing over this man's body, knife in hand, covered in blood I realised what I had done. What if he had family or children? I'd murdered their dad! It wasn't my fault, if he had not broken into my house he might still be alive. I wasn't thinking!
I was arrested soon after, but was found not guilty as it was deemed as self-defence but I still hear his voice echoing in my ears. It's driving me completely insane!

Jess Mugglestone (14)
The George Eliot School, Caldwell

THE UNSOLVABLE!

I'm Detective Willson and this is my story...
I'm working on this case and have found very few clues. A torn piece of an old leather jacket on a rusty nail, a broken window and a blood-red footprint. The victim's dead eyes stare into space showing the terror of their final moments. A pool of blood lies next to the discarded knife with one clear print. I already know whose fingerprint it is. Mine... but I wipe the print away and burn my shoes. I think to myself, *nobody will solve this because I am the detective and the KILLER!*

Amelie Atkinson (12)
The George Eliot School, Caldwell

SPY MISSION

What had just happened? I'd been called to a special science lab for a secret spy mission. You see, I was perfect for this, as I was only an unsuspecting boy and the enemy would only see me as lost and lonely, while I wandered the streets. In fact, I was sneaking through a dirty, misshapen air conditioning tunnel. And then I wasn't... Somebody had seen me. Bullets were whizzing and fizzing and I was ducking and dodging and scrambling madly back through the dark, dank passage. At this point, I discovered that I was outnumbered. But I survived!

Thomas Elder (12)
The George Eliot School, Caldwell

THE ESCAPE

I think I've escaped!
About one month ago I was put into prison for something I didn't do and it's not fair! Me and my cousin were complained about by security for apparently stealing when I never did! We did nothing wrong so I'm escaping because I don't want to be kept in a horrible place for no reason and I'm sick of it! We'll keep this a secret, but I did steal one small thing. ONE! But I'm escaping because it's horrible here and I think I deserve better! I will speak soon when I'm fully free! Bye!

Isabelle Cunningham (12)
The George Eliot School, Caldwell

HAUNTED

I killed my brother 5 weeks ago today. I miss him, visiting his grave helps but the guilt overwhelms me.

It was raining that day the sky was ill-lit the raindrops felt cold and heavy. Travelling back to my house thoughts filled my head like a bathtub, only I was the one drowning. I received a call someone was breathing breathlessly.

I found myself standing in front of his grave again, my heart was in my mouth... I stared at the empty 12-foot hole. Two deep breaths rolled down my back a tear trickled down my cheek. It was *him*.

Charlotte Hiscock (12)
The George Eliot School, Caldwell

MURDER FAR FROM HOME

A film crew, in the Bahamas, finished filming their episode for 'Far From Home Holidays'. Since they'd worked overtime, their boss (Matt) had invited them all for a drink. It was quite late so the presenter (Kate) didn't stay long for she had filming the next day. She walked back to her hotel room, and had a glass of wine.

The next day when they went to film on the beach, they realised Kate was very late. They phoned her many times but she never picked up. When they got to her room they saw a horrifying sight... Kate. Dead.

Nicole Moseley (12)
The George Eliot School, Caldwell

THE MISSING BODY...

It was a dark and gloomy night, the moon being the only source of light for miles. Walking across the muddy path, I got to the gate which read 'Welcome to the cemetery'. Walking by, I felt a wave of discomfort. Walking down to where his grave was it looked as though it had been dug up. I tried convincing
myself I was just tired, I quickly started walking wanting to leave. That's when I saw it, I wasn't tired. The grave was open and the body was gone. I suddenly felt an unwelcoming inhuman hand on my shoulder...

Hollie Wonzeri (13)
The George Eliot School, Caldwell

SECRETS WORTH A FORTUNE

I never truly knew the worth of secrets until it was too late. The government was always shady, that was a fact. I never knew how easy it was hacking their emails but I instantly regretted it. Human experiments, executions, I was sick to my stomach. I had to warn the masses, I had to tell everyone. But as soon as I'd made this revelation I heard three words: "LAPD, open up." I had no time to lose, I frantically uploaded my research but before I could publish it my back went numb... I fell, dying, with the uncovered secrets.

Joe Ballard (12)
The George Eliot School, Caldwell

MY BIGGEST FEAR...

The suspect was gone... and the victims were gone too! I had never had something like this happen before... We tried looking everywhere, there were no clues anywhere. I thought this was a case that wasn't going to be solved but then I found a clue, it said: 'To find me and the children you need to find the 6th letter in the alphabet, first letter in love, first letter in orange and last letter in floor...' then I guessed... FLORIDA! We went to a location in Florida and heard the screams and tears of kids. We went in...

James Santos (14)
The George Eliot School, Caldwell

ESCAPE!

I could hear the faint sound of sirens behind me...
I was still traumatised from earlier; I remembered leaping
from the shattered barred window as I heard the officers
pounding down the corridor. I'd been locked up for 113
days! I would tally up every minute on the cobbled stone
wall with the piece of flint from under my so-called bed.
Every minute was torture. I had to get out. And here I was...
I could sense them behind me... I had an idea... I was
scared... I swung around, the gun in my hand. I pulled the
trigger...

Kelsi Brennan (12)
The George Eliot School, Caldwell

LIAR, LIAR

I had an alibi... That was the first lie I told the judge. I would never hurt him. Another piece of false information. I shouldn't be a suspect! I should be the star of the show. Summer was my favourite season, 20 years later it's my worst nightmare. Did they find him? I should have hidden the body better. Why am I so worried I've done this many times before. Surely this will be the end of me. A smile was planted on my face as the judge shouted, "Not guilty!" I walked out of court, planning my next move...

Shelby Tonks (13)
The George Eliot School, Caldwell

THE MISSING GRANDFATHER

He was gone, the man we'd only buried a week ago.
Depression was still dragging me down. My grandfather
passed away last week and he wasn't in his grave. I sat in
bed, exhausted. I flicked through my mind and memories
came flooding back, one main one being how my
grandfather would sing me to sleep when I was six.
A few hours later a noise came from downstairs. Being the
imaginary detective I thought I was, I went to check.
Nothing. As I turned to go back to bed, there was humming.
He was humming my favourite lullaby...

Isabel Gudgeon (13)
The George Eliot School, Caldwell

THE MURDER

One bright, early morning at the police station there was a commissioner called Jude Bellingham, he was starting to get comfy, relax and was having a smooth lie-in until the phone rang. There was a girl shot dead at the arena in Barncove. Her name was Marley Jacobson. A well-known girl. The people who heard the gunshot were her parents, Marc and Julie, and her brother Josh. They were on a walk until she went to the toilet and was found dead. Jude was almost convinced it was one of the three suspects and was convinced it was Marc...

Owen Stokes (11)
The George Eliot School, Caldwell

FRAMED

They just don't understand, do they? I'd left all the clues they could ever need out for them, and yet they just couldn't piece it together. Now they think that she, my sister, did the deed. After her arrest they left the case behind and forgot about it, allowing me to get away with murder once again. My partner in crime, however, thinks it was cruel of me to frame my sister, of all people; how foolish. All that matters is that I'm not in jail, now I'm free to choose my next victim. And I know just the person...

Milah Ehsan
The George Eliot School, Caldwell

SOLVED!

I'd found a clue, there was a partial fingerprint on the knife that was at the scene of the crime. That narrowed the suspects down to just five people. I brought the first suspect in and interrogated them, they said that they knew nothing about the crime as they'd been shopping at the time, but the cameras in the shop told me that the suspect hadn't been there at all. The next lead then arrived and told me they saw suspect one in a dark alley five minutes before the crime. At that moment I knew who the murderer was.

Jacob Hardy (12)
The George Eliot School, Caldwell

MISSING DOG

One dark and gloomy night a dog, Buster, went missing. The owners were desperate to have their precious pooch back. Next door felt so sorry for the couple, they'd only just moved into the new house, so they decided to put up posters to find Buster all around the town. The whole town community joined in and searched for him. Eventually, they found Buster next to a lake trying to catch a fish to have for dinner because he was so hungry. Everyone was happy he was safe again. He had a few welcome home presents and tasty treats.

Hollie Lister Farrington (12)
The George Eliot School, Caldwell

MURDER MYSTERY

One gloomy night I looked out of my bedroom window, to see ambulances and police cars across the road. I knew something bad had happened and just moments later I got a call from work saying there had been a death reported and they needed the best detective ever to solve the murder. Within minutes I was over the road looking for clues. I found fingerprints, a gun and footprints leading to the back door. After analysing all the clues there were two possible suspects: John and Mark. I looked even harder and found out it was Mark.

Lilli Langton (12)
The George Eliot School, Caldwell

THE MYSTERIOUS KIDNAP

It just didn't add up! How on earth did someone get into the dark, mysterious black corridor leading to Luna's room. *How did they get there?* she was thinking vigorously. What were they going to do to her? These thoughts kept overflowing her brain and it felt like she was being told what to do and say. These thoughts kept on coming back until she heard a deafening bang! The next minute, she found herself being locked in a room all on her own, with no light and no food. Will we ever find out what happened?

Lucy Gibson (14)
The George Eliot School, Caldwell

THE DEAD CAN TALK

People think the dead can't talk, but in reality, they have plenty to tell us, it's a case of paying close enough attention.
It was clear the body had been lying for a while, the smell alone told us that. A hint of a smile was still on his face, his eyes open, fixed on the ceiling. At first, we thought this was natural causes, until we noticed his index finger had been cut just below the first joint. Why would anyone kill just for the fingertip of Travis Baker? And where were the keys to his office building?

Harper Ward (12)
The George Eliot School, Caldwell

THE GHOST OF OPAL TOWN

I walk, my head hung low and my hand grasping the stems of the dandelions. A bitter wind passes me, making me shiver. I look up, confused. The summer sun has been hidden by grey clouds. I shrug it off as I walk towards my grandfather's grave. I didn't have enough time yesterday to pay proper respects so I have come back today.

As I arrive at the grave I can already feel that something is off. I look to see my grandfather's body missing. As I turn to run for help I am knocked down by a frost-biting mist...

Lauren Jukes (13)
The George Eliot School, Caldwell

MY FIRST MURDER CASE...

Inspector Cerys Attwood here. Today was one of the most important days of my whole entire career. This was the day, where I was to sit down all of my suspects for the murder of Tiana Ross. My first EVER murder case. It was now around 14:00, and I had my DS and officers ready to make an arrest.

As I started my explanation of how the murder was committed, the mother of the deceased was darting her eyes around the place as if to say her being here was pointless, but I knew it wasn't... as she'd murdered her...

Cerys Attwood (11)
The George Eliot School, Caldwell

THE MASS MURDERER

It was around 10pm on a Thursday evening, quite a spine-chilling atmosphere. I was minding my own business when all of a sudden I heard a tumultuous sound. There was a scream coming from flat number 38, so I rapidly ran to see what had happened. By the time I found my way to number 38, it was too late, there was a card on the table with an unknown figure leering at me. I picked up the card and rushed to the police station, gave the policeman the card, and he said, "We've found the mass murderer!"

Gemma Collins (12)
The George Eliot School, Caldwell

THE MYSTERIOUS DISAPPEARANCE

The girl wandered through her new house, her dress flowing behind her. The girl's name was Flora Gardener, her father and mother were away. The year was 1913 so her father was a soldier for the British Army and her mother worked as a nurse. She had the responsibility to look after the garden. She walked into her garden and noticed a small door, as she walked closer, a long pale hand grabbed her by the arm and pulled Flora in. She tried to scream but she realised that nobody was there to save her.

Ava Ellis (12)
The George Eliot School, Caldwell

UNSOLVED DEATH

Last night, whilst I was on a date with my boyfriend, my mother was murdered. My dad was 'away on a business trip', but when I got home he was sat on the floor crying. Today as I woke up I swear I saw my mother standing in my doorway next to my father. Could he be involved in my mother's death? I was worried about staying at my house in case he was, because I could be next.
Today was weird. About an hour ago I got a text... from my mother... but she's dead? What's going on?

Lexie Cooper (11)
The George Eliot School, Caldwell

LIE DETECTORS DON'T LIE!

The lie detector test was back and the suspect was lying. I knew he had done the crime. This all started when Tom (who was the suspect) had stolen from a clothes shop and was caught on CCTV, however when we found him and took him into police custody he just wasn't telling the truth. So later on that day we gave him a lie detector test to see if he had been lying or not and a couple of hours later it came back with a positive result.

Weeks later, Tom was found guilty and was put in prison.

Mollie Haynes (12)
The George Eliot School, Caldwell

THE MASTERMIND

I had found a clue but a useless one though. Due to earlier evidence found at the scene we had deduced that whoever the criminal was he had fled and had left no traces of where. Whoever it was must have had good knowledge of the police if he could find ways to get around our methods and escape, leaving no traceable evidence behind. We have no leads, though we do know that he is a criminal mastermind and that he must be a police officer to know so much about the police and our methods. Who is he?

Rhys Jones (11)
The George Eliot School, Caldwell

ZOMBIES DO EXIST

I didn't believe in zombies until today. I was in the isolated graveyard, seeing my dead mother. The body was gone: all was left was the earth mountained next to the empty, deep dark hole. As the night went on, I saw immense footprints leading out of the bare grave. Then I felt something on my back: it was my mother. A zombie. I had not seen her for years and I could finally see her again. I went over to hug her, but then the green, mutated-like body tried to bite me, and I never came back.

Amy-Leigh Wilson (13)
The George Eliot School, Caldwell

IT LURKS...

Icy fingers gripped my arm in the darkness. I felt him breathe cold air on my shoulder, sending shivers down my spine. A shrill cry echoed in the mist and the moon stood proud in the sky. All of a sudden, thick fog filled the atmosphere and the air turned all around me. Crows were cawing in the distance and I was overwhelmed by fear. The wind howled and my face turned a pale white. My hair stood on end and a lump came to my throat. I turned around, and what I saw would change my life forever...

Emma Hemming (11)
The George Eliot School, Caldwell

THE SUSPECT

Dear Diary,

I was chilling in my office when the phone rang. I answered it. The person said to go to the Shakespeare Hotel. I went there, someone had been killed, her name was Sarah. I went to examine the body, suddenly I saw a strand of hair so I put some gloves on and said to one of the officers, "Take this back to the lab," so they left. I started to talk to some witnesses who were staying at the hotel and one of them said to me that a man was asking where she was all day...

Dylan Holmes (12)
The George Eliot School, Caldwell

THE MISSING SUSPECT

The suspect was gone...

As soon as I woke up I went to check on the suspect but when I got to the suspect's room, I heard the window shatter to pieces. When I walked in, the suspect was gone! I had no idea what to do, I was shaking like crazy and I was terrified. Immediately, I called for help as I was afraid the suspect would harm someone as they were out of their cell now. Back-up came and I was so relieved to see them.

A few days later and still no sign of the suspect...

Marissa Lee (11)
The George Eliot School, Caldwell

CRIME IN THE GRAVEYARD!

As I was walking through the graveyard for a midnight stroll, I saw that a grave had been dug up. I peeked inside the coffin and saw that the body was gone! There was nothing but footprints, I followed them which led me to a man with a weapon and the body was over his shoulder. I was scared to walk closer but I continued and he vanished! I walked back to the gravesite and saw a coffin in the grave so I opened the lid and the body was inside and it was staring at me with wide eyes!

Marshall Glasspool (13)
The George Eliot School, Caldwell

THE INFORMANT

After weeks I've finally got a clue. I came into the station on Wednesday and sat down at my desk, then Detective Miller came over to me saying that he had some news, he told me that one of the boss' henchmen turned himself in and was ready for questioning. I made my way down to the interrogation room and as Detective Miller said, he was sitting in the middle of the room and, to my surprise, he told me everything we wanted to know. We went to their location he gave us...

Erin Spacey (12)
The George Eliot School, Caldwell

HAUNTED HOUSE?

The door creaked... We saw blood on the floor, we heard screaming, we felt like someone was watching us. In the corner of my eye, I saw a light! I ran over to it and I realised we were lost. I held the light up as high as I could, it looked like we were in an abandoned house. Daisy ran into the darkness. All of us had no other choice but to follow her. We saw a giant door. I was curious to go inside. Daisy opened it up. We heard sirens. A lady... We had to run...

Bella Sweeney (11)
The George Eliot School, Caldwell

UNSOLVED AND STILL UNSOLVED

I've solved it... He was poisoned! His body lying next to me cold and white. I look away. I pick up the beer bottle, throwing it in a plastic bag, getting it ready for the lab. Turning round, I feel a cold breeze on my neck. The body has gone... Looking around I feel eyes piercing my skin! I pull my gun out ready to protect myself from any harm but then... I freeze. Seeing the lifeless eyes staring back at me. At that moment, I know I will die tonight...

Chloe Sharrock-White (13)
The George Eliot School, Caldwell

THE BOY

One evening a boy went out with his friends but never came home. His parents started to worry and called 911 to try and find him. When they came upon the boy they discovered something very terrifying...

They went closer, turned him over, he was unconscious with half his face sliced off by a blade.

They started to investigate to see who was the attacker. Still today they haven't found the culprit.

Aimee Morrissey (13)
The George Eliot School, Caldwell

WHERE WERE YOU?

"Where were you when he went missing?" said the detective.

"At the library, checking out a book," I replied, staring him in the eyes, waiting until he was uncomfortable.

"What book were you checking out?" he said, looking at the papers in his hand as if there was something there. But I'd been here before, nothing was on the paper, it was blank.

"Sherlock Holmes," I said smiling at the irony. "Here, have a look."

He took the book, checking the date. "You may go."

Then the flash came again.

"Where were you when he went missing?" said the detective...

Hannah Mills (12)
The Hemel Hempstead School, Hemel Hempstead

THE UNFINISHED LETTER

Nobody was able to discover who she was, not even the best detectives could figure it out. She was a ghost, leaving no tracks of her brutal murders. The latest person she had murdered was Lucas Pritchett, a well-known businessman in the world of riches. She'd slit his throat so carefully, making him feel the crimson blood drip down his throat.
Detectives had gathered around the pale dead body of Lucas Pritchett the next morning, checking the crime scene for any signs of evidence, but there only lay an unfinished letter: 'Ana- '
Detective Fernandez sighed, another useless piece of evidence.

Elvin Fedakar (13)
The Hemel Hempstead School, Hemel Hempstead

THE BASEMENT

"What was that?" I heard a loud bang on my bedroom door. It knocked again and again loudly.

"Mummy I'm scared, I think I see a monster!"

I opened the door and went to my daughter's princess pink decorated room. I stopped as my eyes filled with tears as I remembered that she went missing years ago.

"Where have you been?"

My daughter smiled up at me and said, "The men in the coats cared for me down in the basement while the monsters were trying to eat me."

I stared at her and said, "We don't have a basement..."

Hollie Smith (12)
The Hemel Hempstead School, Hemel Hempstead

UP IN FLAMES

I'm here, standing outside my burning house, wondering what had happened.

The firefighters said they couldn't find the cause of the fire. All I remember is being woken up by my brother, hearing screams and shouting outside. Apparently, it was not a naturally occurring fire, it had been done deliberately by another person. Who would do such a thing? The only thing I know right now is that I want revenge. Sweet revenge. My mum says she has an idea of who might have done this horrible thing. But I'm still here, standing outside my burning house. The mystery remains unsolved.

Amy Warren (12)
The Hemel Hempstead School, Hemel Hempstead

THE WIND IS SILENCE

"Shadows of the looming trees peer down at me, a figure of a tall man is staring right into my eyes from the distance. He keeps coming closer. His cloak covers his face. I can't identify what he looks like. Only an eerie silence surrounds me, the devastating wind that had just ruined the town suddenly stopped once he appeared. He's here. I can't run, all the exits are..."

She had finished reading their only lead for the investigation. Wind rushed past her, and yet, it suddenly started to settle. Soon, only an eerie silence was left. She turned around...

Emily Simpson (13)
The Hemel Hempstead School, Hemel Hempstead

THE PENTHOUSE MURDER

All three suspects have gone missing and one witness has been shot and another stabbed. Who did it? Was it the creepy scientist whose DNA was found at the crime scene? It could have been the psychopath student that has had 32 detentions this year. Or was it the rich businessman who is known to want other people's wealth? MI5 took them all into questioning but they refused to comment. The crime took place just outside the businessman's penthouse but CCTV showed all 3 supects walking past the murder around 6:30pm. That was when the murder happened. Who was guilty?

Rory Barber (12)
The Hemel Hempstead School, Hemel Hempstead

THE RITUAL KILLINGS

27th July 1854,
The murders had all been the same. A bullet shot through the heart and a vicious blade to the head. The gun was a pristine silver pistol, a manifestation of his blighted image of a perfect society. The knife, jagged like his fangs, used to rip through flesh and tear into guts. The summoners make a hollow star painted fresh from the victims' bright red blood. For every body found, there was another child murdered somewhere on the other side of the city. They were trying to summon the one all fear the most. They're summoning... Satan.

Aaron Tapimene (13)
The Hemel Hempstead School, Hemel Hempstead

LAST ONE STANDING

I woke up to a blinding light. I'm not sure how I woke up - I'm pretty sure I had died earlier on. Was I dead but alive at the same time? I wanted to find out, I had to return to the battlefield. I needed to be the last one standing.

Once I arrived I started fighting instantly, but it felt different... I felt invincible. I knew I had my ex-best friend coming my way and the spoilt brat she was, deserved to die.

"Hey bestie!" she withdrew a knife.

I grinned mischievously.

"You can't kill what's already dead!"

Alexis Armson (12)
The Hemel Hempstead School, Hemel Hempstead

A WHISPER IN THE DARK

The dead can't talk, that's what I used to think. Of course, I was wrong. I regret everything I did that tragic night. Alone, I watched the red liquid ooze from her stomach. Tears dripped from my eyes and her deafening screams still rang in my ears. I couldn't turn back now. I stared at her stained face for the last time and sprinted as fast as I could, not turning back. I could hear police sirens behind me, motivating me to continue racing through the woods. I heard a crash in the distance, then her voice... "Hello."

Flori Hudson (12)
The Hemel Hempstead School, Hemel Hempstead

THE EYES OF A KILLER

I'm running out of time. She knows I saw. I'd better explain...
It was a dinner party and I was seated next to her. We were
on a table of four, one in the bathroom. I bent to get
something and when I straightened up, I saw. She was
slipping white powder, arsenic, into his drink. Very quickly,
very discreetly, but I saw her. We locked eyes. Her eyes
seemed to penetrate my soul. I ran. I knew I should have
saved him, but her eyes scared me to death.
It's too late, she's here, she's coming! The murderer is-

Ella Tremayne
The Hemel Hempstead School, Hemel Hempstead

THE WITHDRAWAL

Two years ago today me and my friend Tyler robbed Gregsbank.
13:00. We arrived in our van and we went into the alleyway, I disabled the camera causing an employee to come out and check it. I whacked them around the head and stole their uniform. I dumped the body in the dumpster. I used their keycard to look around and that's when I seized the chance to grab his vault keycard. I went down to the vault room and KO'd the security. That's when I swiped the card, filled the bag and bolted out as Tyler started the van.

Ramone Hibbert (13)
The Hemel Hempstead School, Hemel Hempstead

FALLING

Falling is a strong word... this felt more like slipping, slipping away into the descent of the deep abyss of the extensive ocean. You're floating and drifting closer and closer to the sandy sea floor. It's not just your body; it's your mind. As Maria slowly drifted towards the floor, she didn't yet know when she would hit. She could only think to herself, *what happened?* The answer felt like it touched her mind. Her breath ran out as she hit the soft sea bed. Her eyes closed for the last time in her life.

Emma Lewis (13)
The Hemel Hempstead School, Hemel Hempstead

MYSTERIOUS LESSON

On the 21st July 2004 at 8:30am school started, students were going into their lessons. I was late arriving at 9:04, I walked through the entrance, lots of stuff was very weird, such as no one about walking on the premises, nevertheless I walked in and walked to my lesson.
I walked into science, only the teacher was there. All the bags were there but no people. While walking to my seat the teacher locked the door. This made me very suspicious. Then chills went down my spine, seeing body bags, so I ran for my life...

Thomas Twine (13)
The Hemel Hempstead School, Hemel Hempstead

DAWN OF 16TH

They say the dead can't talk... I disagree. I too once thought that their voices aren't real, that everyone was lying... until I experienced it myself. They haunt you and follow you and never leave you alone, ever, especially on the dawn of the 16th day of every month. It is the time they try to convince you to join them. "We could be friends," they'd say. That's also what she told me while wiping the blood off her knife with a smile. "We can be best friends forever and ever now."

Anja Mudrinic (13)
The Hemel Hempstead School, Hemel Hempstead

THE UNSOLVED MYSTERY OF THE PRESIDENTIAL CRISIS

One day the world changed... It was not for the better but for the worse... THE PRESIDENT OF AMERICA HAS BEEN MURDERED!
At the crime scene they found the weapon that was found was a Glock 19x with a silencer on the end. It was lying on the windowsill of the Oval Office facing the body of the president who had fallen to the floor face first. They first went to everyone that could get into the White House but none of them were the murderer. All their alibis checked out, none of them were the suspects anymore...

Alfie Hedges (12)
The Hemel Hempstead School, Hemel Hempstead

IT ALL WENT BLACK

I held the knife, shaking, thinking, is this what I really want? Suddenly it all went black.

I woke up, phosphorescent lights and people standing over me. My uncle was in the bed next to mine, a knife in his lower leg. Like I had been shaken, everything came back to me. I vividly remembered sneaking up the stairs in my uncle's mansion. Of course, he gets to be rich. I knew I had to kill him, but I couldn't. I don't know why. Mum said I had to do it because I was just little. How wrong she was.

Martha Morris (11)
The Hemel Hempstead School, Hemel Hempstead

POLICE CHASE

It was the night after a case for murder, another police officer was taking home the suspect. As the woman in the car realised he was taking the suspect the wrong way, she followed him for ten minutes and he took a turn to go into the lake. A few seconds later she slammed the pedal and could see someone splashing in the car in the distance. The woman drove to see the suspect dead in the water, the police officer was nowhere to be seen and was gone. Days later, they still couldn't find the cruel man.

Seb White (13)
The Hemel Hempstead School, Hemel Hempstead

MURDER IN THE GENES

It was a cursed family...
They were just an ordinary family of four and they lived in a derelict town full of crime. Many murders were going on in this horrid place, with the same pattern. Litbond were determined to find this killer. Despite this, the family all sat on the aged sofa for film night. The dad said he had a 'special' film to show the family. And instantly it said 'I must carry on what my father started'. His father was known as the 'Nightingale Strangler'.

Archie Hendery (13)
The Hemel Hempstead School, Hemel Hempstead

YOU WILL BE OKAY

Beads of sweat raced down his forehead as he went to check one more time if she was okay. Blood was gushing everywhere, seeping through the wooden floorboards. "Mother you're okay, aren't you?" Moving the hair from out of her face, her eyes were revealed as she stared into nothing. "Mother I didn't hurt you, you slipped didn't you?" Desperately he shook her dead body, trying to wake her up. Red blood splattered all over the walls, all over him.

Holly Jewell (13)
The Hemel Hempstead School, Hemel Hempstead

TELL ME NO LIES

"Guilty!" she yelled.

Never an unsolved case! Always proven guilty! Emily Bates. Job: the best detective ever. Presently solving the murder of five families. But has she got anything to hide?

At HQ, Emily was going over the evidence pointing towards Freddy Bates. There was a knock on her door the person came in. It was her brother Freddy seeing how the case was going. Emily explained everything she'd found.

Later, they were both in court. Freddy was guilty. Or was he? A week later, the truth was revealed.

"Freddy Bates innocent and the murderer Emily Bates!" called the judge.

Isabel Randall (12)

The Purbeck School, Wareham

SHUT EYE

Swish. Tumbleweeds drifted lazily across the dry sands of the west. 'No Return' plastered the walls in faded graffiti. A man dragged his feet across the sand, heading into the town before him. At first it was a mirage; thirst attacking his throat, heat blazing like fire through his veins, cracking his skin. He passed a dusty, old house, the windows were shattered and inside was trashed. The cracked remains of glass showed him his reflection: dull, drowsy, dead. Eventually, he reached a saloon. Inside, he bought a drink but someone had come behind him. "Shut eye," she said. Black.

Annabelle Jakubas (12)
The Purbeck School, Wareham

THE BOY IN THE CHIMNEY

I was him. The guy who found him. I'm surprised I didn't see him before. My name's Chuck Murphy, and what I'm about to tell you is horrible. I'll tell you from the start.
I got news that there was going to be some property development around my area so I decided to destroy my little shack to help out. I hadn't used it in ages. I started with the chimney. Then I saw them, two mummified feet sticking out of the chimney. I called the police straight away.
I found out that the boy was called Josh Maddux.

William Douglas (12)
The Purbeck School, Wareham

MONSTERS LIVE

On a cold winter's night, I was sat in my room when my dog was barking and growling at the door. I was so confused about what I should do so I decided to go and look outside, but there was nothing. The next night he did it again but this time he wouldn't move and just kept barking so I decided to look out my bedroom window. It was there, a creature, just staring up at me. I called the police. It smiled at me. It started to move closer. It broke into my house. "Sir?"...

Benjamin Sharp (12)
The Purbeck School, Wareham

YOU THOUGHT I WAS GONE

"Dead!" This was announced on the 7th September, 1945.
Ten years later, one problem... who did it?
I'm on the run, where do I go? Ten years ago I murdered an innocent woman. The detectives are bringing back the case. Nobody knows this but I killed them, I murdered the women. Will this case ever be solved or will it be our little innocent secret?
When the body was discovered everyone pointed their opinion towards my unstable ex-boyfriend but in reality, it was me...

Faith Welch (12)
The Purbeck School, Wareham

THE REAPER

01:30am

The boat skids across the water as we begin to reach the beach. All of our eyes set on one thing, the darkness of the night conceals us and makes it easier for us to approach.

"Brandon, we will be there in 45 seconds."

"Copy. Echo-4, you're on me."

"Understood."

"Bravo-6, you're on me."

"Understood."

The boat makes contact with the shore and all of us depart it. Remaining low to the ground, we stick to the foliage that encompasses the beach. Keeping my eyes focused in front of me, and my ears open... I advance with my partner...

Brandon Davies (14)
The Wren School, Reading

THE DISAPPEARING ROBBERS

On the 12th April a mysterious event happened that nobody could unravel. Thieves broke into London's bank. People there didn't remember what had happened. It was known only that the bank had been robbed.

Police took up this case immediately, but they couldn't find evidence or witnesses. But later on, the bank's workers described what the robbers looked like. The criminals were detained. They said they had come from 2120. It sounded unbelievable so they were put in jail.

One week later they disappeared. It is still a mystery where they are now.

Iryna Suichymez (12)
The Wren School, Reading

911 CALL

A shadow at the door. Breathe in. Breathe out. Hands shaking. Breathe in. Breathe out.
"911, what's your emergency?"
"Hello? Someone's in my garden, help!"
"The police are on their way, but stay on the call."
Silence...
Click.
A creak echoed across the hallway downstairs. She couldn't calm down. Her heart beat louder and louder. "It's in the house," I whispered in the phone.
"Don't worry, the police are near."
Thump, thump.
She took herself closer to the closet. It opened the door.
"Argh!"
"Miss, what's going on? What happened? Helo?"
Silence.
"Bye-bye."
Beeeep...

Maryam Kazemi (13)
Tollbar Academy, New Waltham

THE PAWED ASSASSIN

Blood curls around the dead queen, swallowing her whole with multiple scars etched onto her skin. Investigators crowd around her, analysing the gruesome injuries. It was late in the afternoon when Her Majesty took a stroll with her beloved corgis. But something happened. Something horrible. "Back away from the crime scene," yelled Mr Brown, chief detective. "Judging from the severe scarring, a wild animal mauled her to death. A rogue bear perhaps?" Then suddenly, a cute little dog appeared from a bush, carrying a bloody limb. The dog barked, showing his collar. "It was the corgi." Then he suddenly fainted.

Esmeralda Kokina (12)
Tollbar Academy, New Waltham

THE MYSTERIOUS HIJACKING

He was gone. Four days after the hijacking, a civilian thought he saw the criminal. The police went over to check, he had disappeared miraculously again. The police went to the vehicle that had been hijacked four days earlier to find clues or fingerprints. There was nothing apart from a note that had been left. It read, '5734, 52.6, 7572'. A police officer appeared from the back, he said, "Those must be co-ordinates."
Officer Michael exclaimed, "Of course!"
The next day two squad police went to the co-ordinates. They came across a warehouse with a tall, pitch-black mysterious figure.

Jacob Braithwaite (12)
Tollbar Academy, New Waltham

THE SLEEPWALKING KILLER

It just didn't add up, the clues were there but no suspect! It was confusion that engulfed my mind. "Detective Montalli?" Chris said. "We found something." His voice sounded concerned but not about the job, about me. I followed him to a cobble drive - it looked weirdly familiar. "M-my house?" I stuttered, not knowing what was going on. Chris hunched over with ultra-violet lights shining it onto the porch. "Detective, can I see the sole of your shoes?"
I lifted my shoes nervously to see the tread matched. Then it hit me, I was the murderous sleepwalking killer.

Evie Jacobs (13)
Tollbar Academy, New Waltham

CASE CLOSED

"I concluded that the two are guilty, case closed!" The judge packed his things away and the two 'guilty' people were taken away by the police officers. The 'innocent' woman smiled at the judge's words and began packing away to go on the run. She grabbed her handbag and walked out of the court. The sky was covered by grey quilts. It thundered furiously and she called a taxi. She swiftly went in and found the police after her. "SWORDS headquarters, London." She grinned, and she handed the money. The taxi quickly drove off, leaving the police frustrated and frightened.

Layla Salameh (13)
Tollbar Academy, New Waltham

KILLER HOMEWORK

I'd done it, finally! I went home after finishing my homework. I lay in bed while watching Netflix when my mum entered the room and saw blood on my bed. "It's that time of the month," I explained quickly.

My mother laughed. "Dinner is ready."

I went downstairs and my dad looked like he had seen a ghost. "Someone at your school was murdered," he said with a pale face.

"I-I feel so bad for her family," I stuttered.

"...They never said a gender." My dad looked at me like someone had died. Murder can be classed as homework, right?

Willow Vickers (13)
Tollbar Academy, New Waltham

SUDDEN SHOTS

Walking down the alley quickly, I hear thunder strikes as fast as a blink. The rain pours like millions of butterflies painted whiter, but more dull, eerie, worrying... *Boom! Bash! Bang!* As loud as a siren, gunshots arise. All of a sudden, lots of thoughts tear in my mind. "I know you're there!" somebody says. My heart pounces, I know it. I begin to feel dizzy and unwell. Somebody or something hits me... I'm done for. "Good job boys. We did our job." A man cheers. "Glad to help, I don't care about my sister anyway," someone says happily.

Esmé Kent (11)
Tollbar Academy, New Waltham

PATCHES THE CLOWN

My name? Wouldn't you like to know? John Wayne Gacy, or, as you may know me, 'The Killer Clown'.
Ten years ago...
There's been another murder, Gregory Godzik, 17, we identified him through dental records. Strangled to death with rope. Sargeant, this is the third murder this month. All strangled. All under 20. They could be connected. We could have a serial killer. Last seen by a Mr Gacy. He was hired by Mr Gacy to do some construction work. Not a suspect, he was home all night.
"I assure you, Mr and Mrs Godzik, we'll find whoever did this."

Amelia Sharp (13)
Tollbar Academy, New Waltham

ONE TARGET

Sobs from loved ones, thrills from cops, yet the truth is still hidden. Don't be fooled by a simple ten-year-old human! Laughter filled his lungs and his mastermind brain planning his next hunt. Determined to make evil go extinct, intimidating others to do his work, no limits in his mind. Cops' heads blowing up with frustration. Fugitives laughing and determined for this to never end, however, they don't know his overall plan. Target after target, criminal after criminal so easy like a row of dominoes. No pattern but one target: destroy all evil. Don't underestimate his skills!

Felicity Green (13)
Tollbar Academy, New Waltham

THE MYSTERY

It was a dark, spooky night. Blood! Blood everywhere. Only security footage was there. No one else was there. No one was near. The cameras only caught the murderers scrambling away on motorbikes. Lights. Flashing lights everywhere blinded me with fear. Tears of people distraught filled the misty air. It was just then the blinking blue lights saw it. The body. The damage. The murder weapon. Questions were asked and answered. People in and out of jail with statements and reports. All different but they all had something in common. Everyone said someone about a bloody knife and teenagers.

Chloe Jackson (11)
Tollbar Academy, New Waltham

THE TESTIMONY

The Warren residence, 1936. The detectives assigned to the case are Norman Willson and Tommy Angelo. Norman enters and tries to flick on the light, failing to do so. He walks away in defeat. Tommy flicks up a light from a nearby candle and whispers, "A nice home to be killed." Norman shoots him a look.

"Get out!" the demonic growl commands. Both detectives are trapped inside. Then, a shadow emerges. Norman is thrown against the edge of the stairs and screams as his own gun fires into his chest. Dead.

That was Detective Tommy's testimony at the trial.

Jared Brewin (12)
Tollbar Academy, New Waltham

"I'M NOT GUILTY!"

"Guilty!"

It just didn't add up. As DCI Swanson was led down to her cell, she was terrified of what would happen next. On discovering the crime scene, she had interrupted a kidnapping and the suspect fled. Blood smeared in the car, DNA samples and personal items from the victim. How could they not see she was being framed? The OCG had planted evidence leading to the court drama and prison sentence as a corrupt officer. "Surely it's better then being six feet under, I should never have fallen in love with such a vile man. An OCG criminal lord!"

Faith Swanson (12)

Tollbar Academy, New Waltham

THE MISSING CHILDREN...

On the 31st October 2018... the night of Halloween. Luna and Harry were alone, trick or treating. A bucket full of sweets. Suddenly, they were swept off their feet. A cloth in their mouths and a hessian bag over their heads. Who was the suspect? Nobody knows. There were two suspects for this crime! But who? James or even Matt. A trail of sweets left behind...

1st November, Matt was snooping around, looking suspicious near the incident... covering his tracks perhaps? Screaming was heard. Matt ran off. We followed. It led to a wood. It didn't look good! *Boom!*

Matilda Cuthbert (12)
Tollbar Academy, New Waltham

WHISPER OF SILENCE

The sound of the police cars' sirens screamed through my body as I showed my badge to the officer and bowed underneath the tape. There it lay, cold and motionless, the body, in the pouring rain. Paramedics ran to get equipment, ushering the bustling crown away, while multiple police and TV cars showed up. "It's all part of the job," I muttered to myself.

As I approached the crowd and body, the surrounding people moved, like I myself had caused this tragedy. I knelt on the concrete and placed my hand upon the body. Then it happened... its eyes opened!

Eva Summers (11)
Tollbar Academy, New Waltham

THE LAST PETAL

Scarlet-red blood trickled down her face. This wasn't the end. It couldn't be, she thought to herself. Suddenly, she heard a bang. Guards. Approaching quickly she forced herself to get up and crawled up the dark staircase as fast as she could. After a few minutes, she reached an ancient door. This wasn't any door, it was the door to the throne room. "No one has been here for decades," she whispered. Mustering up as much strength as she could, she forced open the heavy wooden door. What she found inside the desolate room would change her life forever.

Anisa Safa (11)
Tollbar Academy, New Waltham

THE COLD-HEARTED KILLER

Footsteps. The only thing that could be heard as I walked into the eerie house. This case was mind-bending. Eyes stared at me. The eyes of the victims pinned open, meaning they had to see the torture they endured. As intimidating as this might seem, it was also intriguing. Determined as I might be, the only remote clue we have is they were all facing a window and that's not even helpful. The hands of the victims tied, maybe a signature of the criminal. They're a mastermind. Maybe they have killed before. Let's catch this deceiving uncontrollable murderer.

Grace Grigg (13)
Tollbar Academy, New Waltham

TARGET ACQUIRED

Friday the 23rd August 1987. The sun had laid its head for the good, and the night was young. Two lifelong friends planned a once in a while gathering. Religiously they met at a poky cafe in the midst of an unapologetically urban side of Texas. Smalltalk passed swiftly, and one of the men proposed a gift, a typical brown paper bag. "It's heavy," he remarked with a warm smile. As he opened the bag the warm air froze, as he appeared washed out and pale. "You are under arrest!" Betrayal and disappointment flared through his eyes. It was over.

Alex Reed (11)
Tollbar Academy, New Waltham

THE MURDER OF TOM

There was a murder last night, my friend, Tom. Lights went out and he was stabbed. We heard the door slam shut and a note was left behind saying: 'Who's next?'
I started interrogating, Jerry was confused, but he only spoke Spanish. So I ruled him out. Kate and John were with us all night at the party. I'd found a clue. A card from Kate matching the handwriting on the note. We confronted her, she confessed. She'd tricked Jerry into getting her a knife for the cake, but it wasn't for that, it was for Tom's murder! Case closed!

Chloe Whitton (13)
Tollbar Academy, New Waltham

THE MYSTERY MURDER

Five years ago, in the village of Waltham, a little girl aged ten was brutally murdered in the woods. Her family pledged for the case to be thoroughly inspected. Finally the FBI started investigating. They went to the people living in the area and gathered them as suspects. Then they started inspecting the gruesome body. Suddenly, an FBI agent found a dagger with what they think was the girl's blood. They immediately took a sample of it and tested it then tested all of the suspects and realised there was a match! The suspect David was locked up forever.

Jack Walton (12)
Tollbar Academy, New Waltham

THE BEATING

It was the early 1800s. A small town had just built a new workhouse. At the heart, an imposing treadmill. The power of four men was required to run it. A wicked matron saw the treadmill. Incredibly jealous of a beautiful inmate, matron tied her to this huge treadmill at the dead of night. Tearing her clothes. Blindfolding her. Covering her mouth. In a bid to cancel out her beauty, she flogged her until the poor maiden's blood ran freely and was black under her skin. Punishment? The evil, cruel matron received four months in prison for this vicious act.

Hannah Collins (11)
Tollbar Academy, New Waltham

THE SMILING LAWYER

The lights of the courtroom lit up. The judge cleared her throat. The room went silent. "Wybie Jones, accused of mass murder of nineteen individuals. Do you plead guilty or not guilty?" she sternly questioned. He fiddled with his hands, getting gradually more nervous, then looked to me. As his lawyer, I defended him and pled his innocence. I truly believed my client was an innocent man...

Time went by, and before we knew it, the case came to a close. Wybie was guilty. I smiled while walking to his execution. After all, it was my own crime.

Evie Newton (13)
Tollbar Academy, New Waltham

THE REAL KILLER

I had an alibi, but everybody knew it was me. How could I go on...? But... The gun. I didn't shoot it. Nothing added up. I'm the 'killer' but it wasn't me who shot. The bullet came from a separate angle. I had to find the real killer.

"Guilty!" I couldn't believe it. Imprisoned for 25 years. But on the second strike of the judge's hammer, I had an idea. As the victim was shot, in a flash on of the women left the room. That was it!

"I demand a lie detector test!"

The results came back....

Alfie Wood

Tollbar Academy, New Waltham

TRIGGER HAPPY CRIMINAL

On an early spring morning James Smith, a bounty hunter, roamed the streets looking for a suspect. Shots rang out, James ran to the corner. It was his suspect! James pulled out his service weapon and started firing back, shot after shot. His suspect was fleeing. James got up and gave chase, the suspect leaped from roof to roof but James wasn't far behind. James didn't give up until eventually he found that he had the suspect trapped. James pulled out his taser and ordered him down. He arrested him and took him to the station to be arrested.

Alexander Hanks (13)
Tollbar Academy, New Waltham

WRONGLY ACCUSED

Stood in a room, surrounded by suspects. One of them did it, but which one? They all have criminal records, some worse than others. But they're all here for the same crime. Which one did it? It's like a cat and mouse chase; nevertheless, in the end, the cat always wins. Looking at them all, I think these are all very different people but similar in many ways - maybe it's because they're all criminals? Or maybe it's because they're all wrongly accused. You see, I was the one who did it. I am the one who's behind it all.

Leila Gilliatt (12)
Tollbar Academy, New Waltham

THE TEDDY BEAR KILLER

I left the station to attend to the crime scene. Arriving to horror that no eye should behold, tape swallowed the entire building. Five bodybags, splattered blood marks, stuffed bear organs scattered across the floor with burn marks. Without a doubt the teddy bear killer had done this. No fingerprints appeared, but there was still a mass murderer on the loose. It seemed impossible. Did they even put their soft, vicious hands on the scene? It was a remote detonation. I held up a shard of the detonator. It was a military-grade bomb. It was a clue.

Edward Byrne (13)

Tollbar Academy, New Waltham

HOUSE OF HELL

People think that the dead can't talk, but there is always a voice in the back of my head of my dad who was murdered last year. The cops turned the case cold, however I was still intrigued. Deciding to take this case on by myself was a good idea, well I thought. Clambering through deadly bushes to the house of hell, I reached the abandoned place - the desolate area. The window was already slightly open so I climbed through onto unstable floorboards beneath me. I gazed upon an intimidating woman, who clenched a pistol tightly in her hands...

Claudia Kelly (12)

Tollbar Academy, New Waltham

THE EMPTY APARTMENT

It started when a woman mysteriously disappeared. The police searched her apartment, there was no trace. It was assumed that she was already dead. But was that the real story? Nobody decided to find out. Nobody but detective James. He checked the door but not a pair of fingerprints other than her own were traced on the handle, which was weird as she lived with a roommate who said she was at work all day. The detective went to the roommate's work and asked the manager for her schedule. Apparently, she no longer worked there and had moved...

Amelia Targett (12)
Tollbar Academy, New Waltham

THE LONELY HIGHWAY

The lonely highway. The legend tells that the highway was once haunted by the scarecrow of Highway Cottage. The legend tells there were five girls walking down the highway when they were taken by the scarecrow. Since then there have been numerous search parties but never to be found were the five girls. Every year since, there have been an extra five girls taken. Until, five months ago, twenty-five rotten girls were found hanged on a tree in the garden of the Highway Cottage. If you are reading this, you will be my next victim! Just you wait!

Jack Newby (12)
Tollbar Academy, New Waltham

DARKNESS

No one gave her a warning. She saw her friends running away from the sea, then darkness. Five years later her friend Daisy went back. She saw a figure standing on the rocks. She recognised the figure and ran really fast, shouting her old friend's name. She had run too far. The waves were crashing and her other friend Lila was shouting at her to come back. She tried but then darkness. A few years later Lila saw two familiar figures across the road while it was raining. She ran and didn't look back. There was beeping, then darkness.

Melissa Plater (13)
Tollbar Academy, New Waltham

HELPLESS

Eyes bloodshot, hands trembling, I glanced behind me to see nothing but empty road and an arched tree sheltering a tiny bridge. Stood in confusion, I turned around. Still nothing there. I looked like a zombie as the rain dripped down my face, smudging my mascara to my cheeks. Dread and horror scared my face as I heard a wet crunching footstep behind me. My heart raced but I didn't. Telling myself to move. Telling myself to go. Hands clasped around my neck. A dark figure. A dark starry night... My eyes glaring at my own helpless body.

Hannah Howden (12)

Tollbar Academy, New Waltham

THE KIDNAPPING

There was once a girl going to a fair with her friends. She went into the funhouse except she got lost which made it a lot less fun. One moment later... boom! She was gone, she was kidnapped.

A few months later she was reported dead. The whole town was wondering what happened to the poor girl.

One day, a man went into the station, his name was Nick. Nick was being accused of the murder.

It was court day and Nick was nervous because he said he didn't do it. "I have an alibi!"

He's still on the run...

Eden Castle (11)
Tollbar Academy, New Waltham

IS THIS THE DAY...?

I'd finally found a clue. What I had been hoping for the past six years. Kacey Johnson's body had been discovered in a lake from the place she was living. It just didn't add up! We had searched around here multiple times and nothing had been suspected. Maybe she had only just been put there. As soon as I could, I searched around and I could see something suspicious. A man holding something. I rushed to my phone hoping for back-up. But no. There was no reply. I turned around and the man was stood there with a bloody knife...

Sophie Clarke (12)
Tollbar Academy, New Waltham

THE DREAM KILLER

The dream killer on the loose. The holy grail of wanted fugitives has escaped from the haunted walls of juvenile prison. This woman has a towering shadow of eight feet and has the hiding skills of a small child playing hide-and-seek. This woman is a rotten human being and killed my family. I must put her where she belongs. Don't let this mind-bending monster deceive you into thinking my streets are unsafe for they are not. I will put all my blood and sweat into this investigation. I am Harry Edwards and I will catch this crook.

Harry Edwards (13)
Tollbar Academy, New Waltham

DEATH

Monday morning, I head out to arrest Phil Marly as I'm a bounty hunter. We arrive and swoop in at gunpoint and shout, "Come outside!" Phil Marly steps outside and sprints into the woods. I call the police dog handler to find the man. Within a couple of minutes the dog finds an old abandoned caravan with bloody rags everywhere. We know this is serious so we request the FBI. Soon after, a body is found that matches the description of a missing girl. A little while later the man is found dead on the edge of the woods.

Nathan Gibbs (12)

Tollbar Academy, New Waltham

THE SABOTEUR

The lie detector results were back. It was me? But how? I know I didn't kill Claire. The results had to be wrong. I explained to Detective Spriggs how the results must have been sabotaged. There was no hope. I was arrested for the murder of Claire. I had to solve the crime, but to do that I first needed to prove my innocence. Luckily, I had someone on the outside. I thought he'd help me solve the crime. Instead he betrayed me. He was the saboteur. The one who tested me was the saboteur. Now I was totally isolated...

Alfie Winter (13)
Tollbar Academy, New Waltham

THE MISSING ARTEFACT

It was the middle of the night, in a dark alleyway, as a door creaked open. Suddenly there was a smash.

The sun rose. It was 7am as Steve Bobleso woke. He was just going to the museum, when he realised that one of the artefacts was missing. He called his friend Jerry (who was an investigator) and told him about the break-in.

After the investigation, there were three suspects: Liam, Barry and Zach. They all were the same height as the robber but one thing the robber had was a big scar on his knee. It was huge...

Lucas Tuplin (11)
Tollbar Academy, New Waltham

WANTED AS A SHADOW

Darkness. That is all you see when you run. No home. No place. Nowhere is safe.

This incident has changed my life. I was accused of murder of my own brother. I am truly innocent. It was in the darkness of night. The glass shattered, someone entered the house. All I heard was fighting, then silence. Then police entered the house. My instincts told me to run and that's why I ran. I have been running for a couple of years. Like a shadow in the dark. I have travelled the world while running. I might give my life up.

Dylan Westerby (13)
Tollbar Academy, New Waltham

STABBING IN PLAIN SIGHT

There's been a lot of murders recently and so they hired me to look into it. I have recently heard that the murderer tried to kill someone and failed, we are in court with the victim and suspects. It was difficult to know who did it because it was a very guarded area. Luckily the victim survived the stabbing. Now this is where the work begins. We start to investigate the suspects and I'd found a clue. The victim had a ripped red shirt where he was stabbed. One of the suspects had a piece of red fabric. Guilty.

Luke Johnson (11)
Tollbar Academy, New Waltham

CRIME LIFE

My life changed on one mistake. I became one of the FBI's most wanted. I also became a hideous drunken wreck, but my brain never stopped me. Stealing and murdering is what I did, but not every story has a good ending.
"Guilty."
Before I knew it my new home was concrete and metal bars. Sadness took over me and sadness told me what I was going to do. There's no such thing as prison paradise. Suddenly, freedom was not friends with me anymore and now everything was closing in on me...

Joshua Corken (12)
Tollbar Academy, New Waltham

THE FRIDGE MURDER

I walked into the dim room where a supposed murder happened. A putrid smell tickled my nose. My first thought was to look around the room, but I turned my attention to the fridge, dripping in blood. When I looked inside, what I saw wasn't food but instead, parts of the victim's body. I felt like I was going to throw up when I saw the decapitated head in the fridge, however, her whole body was not inside the fridge, so where could the rest of the body be? Suddenly, I felt a sharp pain in my back.

Julia Gussmann (12)
Tollbar Academy, New Waltham

THE BABYSITTER

This is the story of the strangest night in my entire life. I was going to babysit my best friend's cousin. It was 5pm and my mum had dropped me off. I did what I would usually do - went through rules and times and then went to see little Daisy. She looked at me and went pale. Her parents left and I offered to play with her. She screamed and ran off. That night I saw things. The lights would flicker, while Daisy would not come out her room. Her parents arrived home, she smiled and I quickly left...

Nuala Stephenson (12)
Tollbar Academy, New Waltham

UNSOLVABLE

Knocked out and wounded, waking up to an eerie sensation in my body. Sirens filled my ears, getting questioned on how long I was saturated in my own blood. Looking for my phone in my slashed coat. Oh I wish I never wore my new coat, all I wanted to do was see my friend. Day after day in a hospital bed made me distraught. I was never able to move again. I'm never going out alone, I never want this to happen to anyone. I'm still wondering to this day who did this to me. This crime is unsolved.

Harvey Jensen (13)
Tollbar Academy, New Waltham

MOONLIGHT MURDER

Moonlight, perfect time to strike for a murder. Am I right? Such an easy time to hurt, but no. I'm no here to do that. I'm here to fight it, not do it myself. Time to fight. One down, two down, now time for three. We need to find them! This corner, that corner, time to rush. Not found. I can't stop, this is my job at stake here! I cannot lose it. Another corner. There he is! Run, run. I can't stop. Out of breath, he turns around and stabs. I fall. It hurts. I feel weak...

Oliwia Tyczynska (13)
Tollbar Academy, New Waltham

NO ONE CAN WIN

As I swiftly turn the corner, my suspect Dr Raptor has vanished into thin air. All I can see are the remains of his stolen car. *He's gone off with the jewels,* I think to myself. But all of a sudden I hear an engine starting up, I turn around and Dr Raptor has gone off on my brand new state-of-the-art motorbike with the crown jewels. In that moment I think I have failed my mission. Then I have an idea. I call the agency for some back-up but there is no answer. How can I win?

Holly Clifford (12)
Tollbar Academy, New Waltham

THE MYSTERY OF THE MISSING ENERGY DRINK

One morning I woke up thinking I'd have an energy drink to annoy my teachers at school, but when I looked in my fridge it was gone! It was the worst day ever. I looked all over the house from top to bottom, nowhere to be found. Texting all my friends, they hadn't seen it. I was so upset because I planned this for weeks to annoy my teachers, and I needed it for my collection. I looked over and over again. I got in the car, drove to school and found my teacher drinking my drink.

Alisia Smith (14)
Tollbar Academy, New Waltham

THE END

People think the dead can't talk, but they can. I had taken her life for no other reason than I could. I hit her over the head for my own amusement and slung her away like she was trash. That was three weeks ago. I did not feel anything, nothing.
Now she's in my dreams, haunting me, torturing me. Everywhere I look she's there, her presence suffocated me. I can't take it anymore. It's driving me crazy, her bloodstained face talks to me, telling me to end it...

Lexi-Jo Penney (11)
Tollbar Academy, New Waltham

FALSE ACCUSATION

I had an alibi but these freak shows don't care. Put on death row for murder. A shadow lurks at the cell door. Crawling through this rat-filled tunnel with rotten fumes filling my veins. I had an uncontrollable urge. I had to find my next victim. These heartless hinds put me in here for no reason... well, I'll give 'em a reason. My mind determined. I don't know why but the urge pulls me. Old and rich, frail and weak. The perfect target. Easy. My victim is here. Death!

Oscar Gibbon (13)
Tollbar Academy, New Waltham

PRISON BREAK

David and his batch of corrupt police officers had been fabricating a scheme to get him out of prison. The plan was going to happen on Friday 13th. The morning came and the plan was put into action. One of the inmates punched David in the face, he was concussed. The police escorted him outside the prison where a pirate ambulance waited. However, word had got out to the police. David took his first look out to the world. His plan had worked. Suddenly, *bang!* They had got him!

Ryan Howie (13)
Tollbar Academy, New Waltham

JUST A DREAM

I opened my eyes... but don't remember closing them.
Although it was a year ago, things still don't seem the same.
As soon as I did it a run of regret filled my body. I saw on
the news that a man was found dead in the exact same
place I was in my dream. As I continued to listen to the
news, where the reporter stood in my home town, I learned
about the facts of the murderer which were chillingly
familiar. I wondered, was it just a dream? Then I heard a
knock at the door...

Lilly Melbourne (12)
Tollbar Academy, New Waltham

WEAPON X

A boy, born different to the rest, but not sure how to hide it, his family left him as a child. He was abandoned, alone and confused, not sure what to do. He had blue skin with marks on him, but that's not all, he has an unusual thing like a power but to him a curse, he can teleport but only if he can see where. One night he had a nightmare that made him attack the Queen of England. This changed his life. The army had seen what he could do, he became a weapon. Weapon X.

Matthew Watson (13)
Tollbar Academy, New Waltham

THE MYSTERY UNSOLVED

It was a rainy day and a boy called Adam was doing his homework. When he finished he looked outside. Then he saw a heist going on outside in the bank. So he called the police. When the police came they said to him, "What did you see?" Then Adam went with the police.

"Wait, there is a dead body here." Someone had been stabbed.

Adam said, "Who is it?"

"We don't know," the police said. "Don't worry we will find the culprit and arrest them for their illegal crimes."

But the police declared the crimes unsolvable.

Sophie Calder (13)
Trinity Academy Grammar, Sowerby Bridge

DECLARED DEAD

No one pays attention to you when you're meant to be dead. One hundred people, including myself (apparently), are dead because I killed them. I wasn't on the run now. Well, not anymore. I was finally free. Finally free to kill. People would call it revenge. I say I'm just repaying the favour, or completing unfinished business. I wasn't always this way. Not always quite this violent. Oh, what a beautiful chaos I had become. No one could help me now. They were dead. When you're dead, there's no coming back. No second life. No do-overs allowed. Until now...

Erin Lillia Conway (13)
Trinity Academy Grammar, Sowerby Bridge

OPERATION PIED PIPER

Did anyone ever tell you that something lost can't be found? Well, they're wrong. Sit back and get ready for this terrifying story of how a young girl is hijacked. It's the 17th November 1942 and children are being evacuated. Some to happy homes, whilst others are thrust into the darker side of humanity. Unfortunately for Eliza, the next chapter of her life is a dark unforgiving tale that will scar her forever. Eliza and her friends are waiting to be evacuated to start a new adventure in their lives. Unfortunately for Eliza, things take a turn for the worst...

Imogen Taylor (13)
Trinity Academy Grammar, Sowerby Bridge

THE ALLEYWAY!

The desolate being, no stranger to multiple crimes over the years, was the centre of attention again. A report came in from a petrified woman saying there was a shriek coming from the gloomy alley. Past the time any sane human would be caught passing by. Buried amidst the half-eaten greasy chicken and mouldy pizza lay a lifeless soul of what appeared to be a young girl. With peeling paint and brown rust, the wheelie bin took on rain and sunshine, witnessing every quiet and loud crime. The mutilated body leaned against the side, tossed away like some rag doll.

Adiba Islam (12)
Trinity Academy Grammar, Sowerby Bridge

WHO WAS IT?

It was twilight, the tranquil waters danced to the tender breeze. My friends and I ambled on the damp sand. *Boom!* We heard the crackle of lightning. Rain started pouring heavily and the sea growled in fury. We pelted to the adjacent abode, it was subfuse and sinister. We turned around as we heard a shrill creaking sound, to notice the door shut, taking away the only natural light. The lights flickered to reveal a pool of blood. My friends lay slain. I looked ahead in dread, in the broken mirror I saw myself holding a blade dripping with blood...

Shrena Ramakrishnan (12)
Trinity Academy Grammar, Sowerby Bridge

HER AND ME

I had this roommate. She was always a wild card. She had problems in the past but this seemed different. Every Sunday she would leave for around an hour and every time I asked about it she wouldn't respond. Maybe she hooked up with her ex or something. Still, I've been her roommate for almost a year now so she should tell me anything. I followed her and I realised she was going to a church. I never knew she was religious. I listened through the door and heard her speaking to people. "I think my roommate is haunting me..."

Phoebe Graham (13)
Trinity Academy Grammar, Sowerby Bridge

THE BASEMENT

I fell asleep at my girlfriend's, her parents were out so it was just us. Around the middle of the night I heard scratches, just thinking it was her cat I went to shut her up until I heard whispers under the floorboards. I went to investigate and took away the board it just showed me the basement, so without thinking that's where I went. I knew this was a mistake but instinctively I walked around and some hobbit-like men jumped at me. I screamed as they grabbed me. "Now get the other one," they said and I blacked out...

Eleanor Baines (13)

Trinity Academy Grammar, Sowerby Bridge

I FEEL NO GUILT, BUT I SHED A TEAR

She hung there, rope tight around her neck, her eyes gouged out and in their places were sunflowers. The sounds of sirens increased and red and blue flashing lights surrounded the driveway. What had I done? I ran into the house seeking shelter; I had become a monster. I had killed my own friend and now she was lifeless and the blood poured down her face like a waterfall, her skin slowly turning a snow-white, being nibbled by the cold, leaving her at one with nature.

"I am a monster," I smiled to myself in the mirror.

Amelia Czapiewska (13)
Trinity Academy Grammar, Sowerby Bridge

HOUSE ON FIRE

I awoke to the fire alarm. I jumped out of bed and looked out of my window, there was somebody I didn't recognise running away from the house. I realised the fire wasn't an accident, this person had done it. I tried to open my bedroom door but I burnt my hand so I smashed through the window and jumped out. I ran after the figure in the distance. I yelled after them but they didn't care. The house collapsed behind me and when the police arrived I was arrested for the murder of everyone I ever knew and trusted.

Lily Roberts (13)
Trinity Academy Grammar, Sowerby Bridge

NOT GUILTY

The police car sped away. The body had been removed. I wiped my fake tears away, the acting class really paid off I guess. I put the knife in his teddy bear. I knew he would be buried with it so I would never get caught.

Three years later I'm still walking free. The guilt has been following me around but I would gladly kill again. The bloodstains are still on my clothes though but why should I care in the words of him: "I am a monster." I showed him the real monster of me. I hope.

Annabel Walker (13)

Trinity Academy Grammar, Sowerby Bridge

DO I HELP 'EM?

A man with dark, curly hair was hunched over on the pavement, screaming, his eyes wide black holes in a pale face. A few feet away, facing him, was another man who was also shouting. He held a long knife in his hand; under the streetlamp light, I saw it was slick with blood. My physical response was immediate; I could hear my heart thumping in my ears and every muscle in my body tensed. Part of me wanted to run away as fast as I could, but another part of me was wondering how to help the poor man...

Elena Mirgova (13)
Trinity Academy Grammar, Sowerby Bridge

FIFTY AND COUNTING

I threw the body into the fire and smirked. Now that the body was dealt with and the carpet was disposed of I could flee. I grabbed the handle of my suitcase and left. 3 - I left the garden. 2 - I climbed into my car. 1 - I prepared myself to go. *Boom!* I drove off, not looking back.

Five months later, 50 more murders. I finally was caught. I was led into the interrogation room. I sat down and they started questioning me. I passed them a paper midway and gave them a sad little smile...

Mehek Ali (13)

Trinity Academy Grammar, Sowerby Bridge

LAST BREATH

Hanna's hands and feet were icy cold and legs so frail she could barely stand. She was repulsed by the stench of her own skin. Her chapped lips and mouth craved water and hair so greasy from the steam around her. Little did she know her suffering had only begun. She had no sense of where she was, the crate she was being held in was swaying left to right as if on the road. In her last moments she was forced to inhale some unknown gas. That was when she knew that would be her last breath...

Aliya Rahman (12)
Trinity Academy Grammar, Sowerby Bridge

MASS MURDERER

"Breaking news: mass murderer Lucas Stern breaks out of prison and is on the run. Police warn to stay indoors. Fourteen incidents have already been recorded in the last seven days alone."
I started to run. "Lucas go away," I screamed into the darkness. I saw his beady eyes approaching me at high speeds and as I ran I thought was my life really going to end here? No it wasn't. I stood and faced my attacker...

Hannaan Arbab (13)
Trinity Academy Grammar, Sowerby Bridge

THE MISSING PIECE

Blood splatted against the wall, a body of a girl with a gun in her hand.

"Obviously a suicide," the inspector said.

"No," the detective replied, "the gun can't stay in one's hand while falling down dead... murder."

The two took the gun to the lab to check the fingerprints but, the test came out void. The inspector looked somewhat relieved. The detective went back to the crime scene to search for clues alone, or so he thought.

"Detective Boyce," a gravelly voice said.

"Hello Inspector Buller."

Bang! The detective was shot in the head by Inspector Buller.

Jonathan Purse (12)

Twynham School, Christchurch

SHERLOCK'S ON THE CASE

Bang! and the hostage was dead, leaving blood everywhere. The next hour, inspectors, ambulances, and detectives all came. The inspectors were trying to find clues, the ambulance took the dead body away, the detectives were trying to find out what happened. Then suddenly *bang!* breaking through the doors came Sherlock Holmes, the best detective in the world, with a straight long face, walking like he owned everything.

"What have you found?" said Sherlock.

The inspector pulled out a used bullet.

"As you can see there are scuff marks, so whoever it was they met someone else!"

Maria Butt
Twynham School, Christchurch

THE HEIST

The sirens went off, bank sirens, emergency sirens. *Bang! Bang!* Gunshots in the distance. Colleagues running with money into the car.

The police are behind us, *skrrrrrr!* The car wheels screech as we go driving into the night, drifting round corners, running red lights.

Hurtling past slow cars and police cars, we drift into a car park, losing the helicopter. We get out of the car and get into another, driving away calmly to not get caught again. We drive to the hideout, collecting all the money, splitting it all, talking about our next heist.

I wonder what's next...?

Ollie Dashwood
Twynham School, Christchurch

WOULD YOU LOVE ME MORE?

Guilt flows freely through my veins, poisoning my once carefree thoughts and threatening to blow my cover. Everything is so chaotic in my brain, reality zooming in and out of focus like a broken camera lens. It's a struggle to separate real life and what my overactive imagination conjures up, but my attempts are forever in vain. My sanity left me when the nightmares unexpectedly began. Horrific images shatter any chance of a restful night's sleep, but the luxury was always far from mine. I thought he'd love me more. Apparently being a murderer isn't as attractive as it seems.

Mya Lonnen (12)
Twynham School, Christchurch

FRAMED

I woke up to a buzzer. It was my time for the electric chair. Today was the last day of my horrible life. The policeman came to me and said, "It's time." I'm here today because of my father, who killed them. I wasn't guilty.
They tied me up. I couldn't move. Tears went down my eyes. I then shouted, "It was my father."
The policemen then said, "What?"
I replied with, "He blamed it on me."
They untied me and said, "We'll talk to you later."
The police came back with some news. Was I guilty?

Dylan Winter (12)
Twynham School, Christchurch

THE MURDERS

My heart skipped a beat. There was no denying the results.
Ever since we found the bloody bodies hidden in the barn, I
knew something was up with him. I should have known.
As I walked into work this morning, I saw his head droop to
look at the floor. He killed my family. How could I work for a
murderer? A liar?
"My boss, Keith Raymond, is the killer. He chopped up my
family and hid them. *It's him!*" I shouted at the jury.
"Before we lock him up he needs an interrogation," stated
the Judge.
"Lock him up!"

Isla Crum
Twynham School, Christchurch

THE SHADOW

Detective Jones had just received an important call. Two people had been killed and dragged into an abandoned cottage near Buckingham Palace. The bodies had only just been found with two deep cuts across their chests. He was now at the crime scene looking for clues. There were no signs of clues around, not even a hair. Suddenly, downstairs he could hear floorboards creaking. A dark shadow had emerged at the door. Knife poised in hand. It took a few steps towards him and a threatening cold drowned him. He gasped for breath, but no air reached his lungs. *Darkness...*

Claudia Spencer (12)
Twynham School, Christchurch

BREAKING POINT

Three photographs were laid out in front of me, graphic details I could not look at. The blood, the crime scene, I winced as the realisation was upon me. Sat in interview room 6, an hour into interrogation, Detective Benjamin Linus approached my face. "I'm going to ask you one final time," he said, then leaned into me and bellowed, "Did you kill my wife?" Saliva sprayed into my face as he roared the question at me.

I calmly took a breath, met his gaze and with a smirk on my face replied, "No, I could never kill my mother."

Sophie Nicholson (12)
Twynham School, Christchurch

THE KIDNAP

I looked out my window, to my surprise the neighbours weren't in. Then a large shadow stepped out the door. My heart stopped. It was a person. They had the neighbours' child under their arm, put them in the car and quickly drove away. I had to do something; I called the police, they said they'd be 20 minutes. I didn't have that long! I went after them myself. The operator said to stay on the phone so I could keep them updated. As I followed them I found myself screaming, "No!" But it was too late. I couldn't help.

Phoebe Bennett (12)
Twynham School, Christchurch

FAMILIAR KILLER

Not a shadow of a body remained. It was an endless abyss of bodies. Dead bodies. The stench of rotten skin was intolerable, the odour of flea-infested blood hung in the air like a stormy cloud of fate. Streams of gushing blood and ribbons of writhing red littered the ground. The moon shone on the pools like a deadly creature's eye. It all made sense now. The three o'clock call. The urgent voice. Shaky pitch. I had merely inferred it was cold. But this was rancid. He had outdone himself, I'm ashamed to admit the work of my brother.

Poppy Miller
Twynham School, Christchurch

CLUELESS

They say a picture paints a thousand words. Well, the picture that stood before my bloodshot eyes would forever haunt my nightmares. The blood, painting the once serene landscape. The solemn-looking family of the victim. The body, insides visible. I never liked the colour red. Growing up, I always saw it as a symbol of sadness, depression, fear. How right I was. The area was searched to the bone for clues by the police yet none were ever found. Luckily for me, the local police force wouldn't find a clue if it slapped them round the face.

Ryley Deacon (12)
Twynham School, Christchurch

TIME TO GO

He's dead, she's dead and I'm dying. Why did I do this report? Corruption. I'm an innocent journalist with that topic. How did I get here? It's my turn to go; so soon. Torture, waiting for his poison to kill me. Feeling my every heartbeat possibly being the last. Why are people so cruel? Wait, I think I hear a muffled whisper outside. "Is he dead yet?"

"No!" I bellow at the top of my voice but it only comes out normally. I have a nose bleed: great. It stops, but I never get to see him. I am gone.

Samuel Hooks (11)
Twynham School, Christchurch

FRAMED!

I thought something was fishy with Jack the day of my best friend's murder. He had stains on his shirt and was being edgy around me. The trouble was, if I told my boss it was Jack that committed the murder he wouldn't believe me as Jack was his favourite employee. I went to consult Jack but he was nowhere to be seen.

I turned on the news. The reporter said, "There've been several stabbings in the town square of Christchurch. This is the man to look out for," then they showed a picture of me. What was going on?

Lucas Hayward (12)
Twynham School, Christchurch

IRREVERSIBLE

The pitter-patter on the soaked gravel path, my hair wet and flattened I watched the droplets dance in the sky. Reflective mirrors rippling around me. The flash of repetitive red and blue and muffled sirens flooded my head. I stood as the cold ice-sharp reality hit me, a reality I fought not to give in to. My vision blurred as I felt the cold metal of handcuffs pierce my wrists. My thoughts were jumbled like a murky lake in which all you can see is your monstrous reflection. I felt humiliated, what I had done I knew was irreversible.

Molly Kuhne (12)
Twynham School, Christchurch

THE CALLING

In the deepest, darkest, depths of the castle where the dungeons lay, a cold wind wailed like a ghost and I shivered from head to toe. The mystery of the calling was still unsolved. It was just after lunch when I heard the call again, but I couldn't make out the words. Was something in the dungeon calling my name? Nobody else had heard a thing. I was alone so I decided to investigate the unknown sounds. As I crept down the stairs using only a candle for light, something cold and wet touched my arm. I froze in fear!

Beth Stewart (12)
Twynham School, Christchurch

THE SUSPECT

Just as I was looking out the window, I got a phone call saying the suspect had gone. They were meant to turn up to court but they didn't. They must have run away. That moment I knew I had to chase after them and hunt them down. I grabbed my bulletproof vest and my gear but I couldn't find the taser. I searched everywhere but just couldn't find it. Suddenly I saw something in the distance; I looked back out of the window. I thought I saw the fugitive so I ran to check the board of suspect information...

Chloe Robinson
Twynham School, Christchurch

A SHADOW AT THE DOOR

One misty morning Detective Sherlock saw a mysterious shadow outside his door. "It must be an intruder," said Sherlock, puzzled. He nervously went to the door with his feet shaking and a frying pan in his hand as a weapon. Then he opened the door with his heart beating with fear. Outside there was a giant man staring at him eye to eye. "Umm, how you doing?"

The giant man had blood dripping down his face. Sherlock gulped with horror. As the giant man came in he had a sneering smile...

Kitty Johnston (12)
Twynham School, Christchurch

THE BURNT SKULL

It just didn't add up, all the clues were too easy to find so now we are back at the beginning, the entire group has been hitting their heads against a wall. Nothing made any sense, no one had made any difference over the last two weeks from when we were first assigned to this mystery at least a few months ago. With all the crime cases that have been happening this year it has been hectic; every person has reported the same clue of every dead body that has been found. A burnt skull on the neck...

Bethany Edwards
Twynham School, Christchurch

THE MYSTERIOUS KILLER

The lie detector results were back... my knees slapped the ground. He had won. I was out of ideas to prove he was guilty. He surely can't get away with murder? I'll have to think of another way to prove he killed her. If I try to investigate I can prove he's guilty. I knew they'd had a fight, but I didn't think it would lead to this. He killed her. I know it. Last Friday she went missing and never came home. She went to meet him in the dead of the night in the heart of the forest.

Aleisha Hughes
Twynham School, Christchurch

THE SHADOW

A shadow at my bedroom window. The time was about 12:45 at night when I saw the shadow. The only way you could get to my window was by the tree that departed my house from my neighbours' and they're the only ones who could get across by using the tree. Then a minute later they shattered the window they were holding a knife that's when I knew I had to run for my life. I managed to get away to the police station but when I and the officers got back they were gone and so was the house...

Leah-Louise Thorn
Twynham School, Christchurch

THE CHASE

I line up the sniper. Ready to take the shot. He falls to the floor blood pouring from his skull, I place the sniper back in the case, strap it to my back and run. Just as I am halfway to my car, the police zoom round the corner. I climb up over a roof of a house and spot the black BMW. I jump, landing on the roof of the car, and dive into the driver's seat, slam my foot down and rocket off down the road, the police close behind me. Dang it, they've caught up with me!

Otto Williams (12)
Twynham School, Christchurch

ON DEATH ROW

Ten minutes. A mix of sweat and tears trickled down my cheek. My heart pounded faster than ever before. My death awaited. I prayed he would tell them the evidence.
The executioner grabbed me firmly by the forearm and brought me to the noose as I struggled, hysterically screaming, claiming my innocence.
"Wait, stop! Don't pull the lever. He's innocent!" he yelled, but it was too late.

Samuel Chapman (12)
Twynham School, Christchurch

THE MISSING FRIEND

It was a cold and windy day, Checker, Harley and Lucy met on the roof of a train station in Nuneaton.

Checker shouted, *"I'm Checker!"*

Harley said, "No one cares!"

Lucy shouted, *"I like chocolate!"*

They went to meet John from the train because they had not seen him for about 3 years.

They started to remember that John had not done anything wrong - ever. They began to plot with each other on the way to the train. *Perhaps I can get him hooked on chocolate*, Lucy thought.

John was never to be seen again...

Wyatt Mainwaring (14)

Values Academy, Stockingford

A NIGHT IN THE WOODS

Tyrone, Steven, Zoe and Lisa all met in the woods on a stormy day.

It was Tyrone's plan to try to stay overnight in the dark scary woods. They saw something running past, Zoe said, "I'm going, I don't like the feeling of this," and walked off. Now it was just Lisa, Tyrone and Steven. Tyrone said, "We're camping for the night" Lisa and Steven agreed

"What was that running past?" said Steven.

Zoe called Lisa and said, "You must get out of the woods now. When I was walking home I got a warning from a strange woman..."

Kaidon (14)
Values Academy, Stockingford

TRAIN CARRIAGE MYSTERY

The train was dark and cold, Detective Jack was alone at the back of the cart with a few other passengers just down the other end. His eyes wandered far and wide, noticing a man he knew long ago. An old friend we'll call it... Jack looked away and within a few moments the windows started to freeze. Jack's hands started to tremble. The cold, stone-hearted detective trembled with fear. His eyes widened. His breathing shaky, Jack's eyes closed to find his old friend just in front of him, the other passengers were gone.
"Where have you been dear friend?"

Cameron Fish (15)
Values Academy, Stockingford

WOULD YOU TRUST THEM?

One stormy night, Abi and Mark met in the woods and the wild wind was howling through the trees. They hatched a plan. They were dressed in Halloween costumes. Mark had red contact lenses. He directly stared at Abi and said, "We will get Leveon and if he doesn't come..." Abi interrupted him and said, "We will force him to do what we want!"
At first Leveon was suspicious but he knew he had to go because Abi threatened to hurt someone he loves.
He woke up on train tracks and heard a noise coming towards him...

Camron Milburn (14)
Values Academy, Stockingford

THE MAN

The door shut behind him. He ran to the door, there was nothing, he was just looking into the void. He kept saying to himself, "I shouldn't have come to the horror house. I'll just look around. Slowly and cautiously..."
He was walking across the hallway and he saw a light in the kitchen. It was a lantern but there was not much left, it must be used carefully. He saw a speedy shadow and he didn't know what it was...
It was a man with blood-red eyes in the eerie, frightening, dark shadows...

Cameron B
Values Academy, Stockingford

IN THE FOREST

Once upon a time, there was a little boy called Jayden, he had autism. He was 15 years old.

One day, it was his mum's birthday. His mum was called Amber, his dad was called Matthew.

After Jayden had wished his mum a happy birthday, she went outside to get some fresh air. When she was standing in the front garden, she heard some really weird noises coming from the forest. Amber called out to her son, "I'll be back in a minute."

She entered the forest and saw something weird...

Elliot Prince (14)
Values Academy, Stockingford

THE HEIST

They met again, the team of seven people, Bob, Jeff, H, Tom, John, Mike and Andy. The team was ready. H was the leader, H looked like this: he had a big white beard, he was covered in tattoos but the bad thing was he was not smart. Jeff was a disgusting man, he was short, he annoyed everyone, he did not help the team. He was only in it for the money. Bob was a brilliant hacker but the cops knew him. Today they worked towards the heist, but their differences proved to be too much...

Jack Goodman
Values Academy, Stockingford

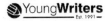

THE ESCAPE

This is about four men: Adam, Roco, Jono and Roger. They were the maddest people in the world! The prison they were in was called The Castle, it was over the sea. Their cell was high and secured and the windows were barred. But Rodger had a plan to escape. When it was night they got out of the cell but the camera saw them and *bang!* Adam was injured. The others were caught and were sentenced to the electric chair. Now escape was even more important...

Harvey

Values Academy, Stockingford

THE MAN IN THE WOODS

One day I was playing in the woods behind my house, then I tripped over a log and fell. When I looked up there was a tall man covered in blood, he had sharp nails but his back was facing me I was eager to escape but I could not shout or scream: I was frozen.
The next day I had a sleepover at my friend's house but then all the cool kids showed up so I decided to leave. I was on the way home about five minutes away when I just froze...

Curtis Lee
Values Academy, Stockingford

WRONGLY ACCUSED

"Not guilty!"
It just didn't add up...
There's just one more piece I couldn't figure out. I recalled vivid visions of blood dripping from his hands as life drained out of Sarah's body. I'm certain there's something else. Untainted silence in the crowded courtroom was followed by the shrieking moans of revolt. My face turned scarlet-red as I couldn't control my anger. It felt like a fishbone stuck in my throat.
Defendant's grin was like a knife piercing my heart. Sniggers underneath his breath and grimaces still lingering in the air. How has it come to this?

Gracelyn Ellis (13)

Voyage Learning Campus, Worle

MORAL DILEMMA

Moral Dilemma.

Morals. Morals make us human. Her head smashed into the wall; justice was complete but my brother's morals had shattered. This was wrong, totally wrong, and truly wrong. My brother murdered a killer. She deserved pain, but no one deserves death. "Nor did the victims," my brother argued. He always spoke honestly, he couldn't survive court without help... and my legal defence. As a lawyer I stand for my clients' freedom. I cannot truthfully protect him on the stand as I know the truth. However family comes first; he is my brother. I pray God forgives me for my act.

Annabelle A
Voyage Learning Campus, Worle

FALSE INFORMATION

I was really confused by the call I'd just had with the police. They wanted me to go down to the police station.

As I arrived, my friend was inside crying. I rushed over asking her, "What's wrong?" She was too distraught to answer.

The policemen asked if they could talk to us. I nodded. They said, "Layla's house was burnt down with her family inside." I asked, "Why am I here?"

"Layla was with you last night so we had to see if this information was correct," they replied.

I was startled because Layla wasn't with me...

Summer Ellis (12)
Voyage Learning Campus, Worle

THE LIE OF HIS LIFE

The lie detector results were back. There was a kid named Pedro and he was peddling drugs at school to other students. A student saw him exchanging drugs for money and he went to tell the teacher. The teacher informed the police and they came to do a drug raid. Pedro hid his stash in the boys' toilets (stinky!). The police searched his desk... no schoolboy should have five hundred pounds in cash in their English book! They bought Pedro into the station for questioning. He said he had been set up. But the lie detector tests were back...

Logan Smith (13)
Voyage Learning Campus, Worle

CAN THE DEAD TALK?

The blue lights pulled up to the scene under the dilapidated water bridge. The witness called it in after he saw a corpse drifting in the water.

Three gunshots in the head resembled that cold case. Stamped x on her wrist. Her cold bloated body looked like it had emerged from the gates of Hell; with eyes piercing into oblivion. Vomit filled my own mouth at the realisation it wasn't over. Echoes of the stranger's statement kept vibrating in my head...

When I turned back the witness had vanished. How did he know so much about her?

Fuschia Vass
Voyage Learning Campus, Worle

TOP COP KILLER

An interview's being conducted at a secret holding facility in London, John Adams has been charged with first-degree murder and possession of an illegal firearm for the murder of Metropolitan Police Counter-Terrorism Commander James Sampson with a gun.

Detective 1: "Afternoon Mr Adams, do you understand why you're here today?"

John Adams: "Yes, I killed one of your own innit?"

Detective 2: "Mr Adams, was this done intentionally and why?"

John Adams: "Yes, I hated his fake plans on solving terror and crime in this great city. He just wanted... *money!*"

Detective 1: "Money from who, John?"

John Adams: "No comment."

Joshua Ssempiira (13)
West Hatch High School, Chigwell

NATURE'S GAME

The forest loomed around me. Crooked tree branches like slender fingers grabbed for my backpack, just missing. Far in the distance was a city full of fog and mist, but little did I know that whatever patiently waited for me, was something that would stain my memory for my whole existence. Many questions swam around and yet the main question that echoed in my head was: *how have I appeared in the middle of this void of dead trees and other plants?* This was an unsolved memory puzzle that shall be a game for nature to solve.

Meghana Pirabaharan (12)
West Hatch High School, Chigwell

WHY?

I was sitting on the roof just as the clock struck midnight with an uneasy feeling in my stomach. It was too quiet! A scream rang through the air and a girl dropped to the ground, dead, blood dripping down from her neck. A figure in black ran away from the crime scene. I climbed down and chased them... Luckily the tiring hours of PE finally paid off, I jumped onto them just as they fell down. Unmasking their hood, my best friend lay there stunned. Before she could explain, the police pulled me up and took her far away.

Amelie Lo Giudice (12)
West Hatch High School, Chigwell

THE MYSTERY MAN

In 1990 John Sean Williams was put in prison for 100 years to life for the murder of his two sons. For the 20 years that John stayed in prison he was a very mysterious character, he had no friends, no enemies, nothing. It was like he didn't exist. Meaning that when he was missing at roll-call on 23rd March 2010 nobody noticed. He slipped through security with ease. The strangest thing about his story is that when security found out they searched for him in their database. But he had never even existed.

Lucas Watts (12)
West Hatch High School, Chigwell

SILENCE

Silence. Everything went silent. Sirens were shrieking, bright red lights flickering as heavy footsteps grew closer and closer. It was over.

A quiet trembling whimper came from the corner of the room. As it grew louder, a sudden agonising screech filled the room. My blood ran cold. Silence. A limp, distorted body was thrust against the wall like a rag doll, leaving a deep scarlet stain against the wall. Silence. The footsteps grew closer, as the metallic odious scent grew more unbearable. As my heart palpitated out of my chest, the heavy footsteps stopped abruptly. There was no more silence.

Eve Clowes (14)
Woodcote High School, Coulsdon

JOIN US

It was the 4th of July. Everybody was stuck inside, being bored. Teenagers were resorting to social media, staring at their phones for hours on end. I unlocked mine eagerly, my notifications were exploding my phone. My stories had all my friends, renamed to the username Kun41. I looked at the stories, they each said the same thing, 'Join us'. I knocked on my friend Alicia's door. No answer. I sent her a message, 'Where are you?' After a few seconds of waiting, she sent a location. The second message popped through quickly, 'Come find us'. I'm coming, Alicia...

Leo Keene (12)
Woodcote High School, Coulsdon

GUILTY

Hollow bones shattering as the crunch of his body overpowered the screams of his soul. The filthy concrete screaming as the body hit the ground. She'd killed him. Trembling, sprinting, deep into the night. Violent cries and shrieking sirens chasing her into darkness.
The vile guilt engulfing her in the nightmare she could not escape. Guilt oozing through her melancholy body, her blood became cold. She froze. Life or death. Prison or death. Staring at the rancid environment below her for one last horrendous time. Her frail fingers gripping onto all she had left. She jumped.

Emma Barron (13)
Woodcote High School, Coulsdon

THE KILLER

Gunshots rang through the night. Shortly after, police sirens were wailing through Brixton's empty streets. A lifeless body lay by an alleyway, no sign of the killer. As the killer walked through a nightclub, none of the attendees realised that there was a killer among them. He walked to the restroom to get rid of the evidence. But, as he turned the corner, he felt a cold metal touch the side of his head. *Blam!* Brains spilled onto the floor, ruining the marble floors. The attendees went silent as a bouncer checked the restroom, but the killer was gone.

Zach Parker (13)
Woodcote High School, Coulsdon

WRONG BODY!

"That's not my son!" screamed Miss Hadley. I couldn't think straight. How can your son get mixed up in another coffin?! I'd never come across something so shocking.

We spent the whole evening checking the morgue for her son, but he wasn't anywhere in sight. That's when it hit me. The burial yard. Eager, I jumped into the front seat of the car and drove there. I grabbed a shovel and started digging at the graves like a maniac. That's when I saw him. Bloody, eyes ripped out, not even in a coffin...this boy had only died that day.

Honey Chard-Latouche (13)
Woodcote High School, Coulsdon

INNOCENT PRANK?

Dancing on the rooftop. It was their night. The rain didn't bother them. Neither did the continuous thunder. She thought they were her friends. Her 'friends' were so drunk that they decided to lock her out on the roof, alone, in the torrential storm. Screaming and slamming her body against the door, she begged to be let in. All of them laughing, watching her tears stream down her face, pleading at the top of her lungs until she stopped. A lightning bolt flashed. The noise was gone. They opened the glass door to see Lia's body, dead on the floor.

Aliyah Khan
Woodcote High School, Coulsdon

IT

Deep red handprints covered the walls. I heard footsteps behind me, slowly creeping up... I felt something rest on my shoulder, slowly turning around, my head was dripping with sweat. All I could do was run. I rushed out of the tunnel...
"There's nothing we can do unless you show us proof that this happened."
I left the police station still picturing 'that' in my head. I kept looking behind me in case it followed me. What was it? Why did it want me? A hand gripped around my neck, blood dripping down. I slowly fell.

Kiera Fricker
Woodcote High School, Coulsdon

CATCHING THE CULPRIT

Argh! The sounds of police sirens and screams. George Small lying dead on the floor. Police storm into the skyscraper in the dead of night. Suddenly a smash of glass and a man gliding down heading towards a van. The culprit Kezzie Small, George's brother, a mass murderer, on the run for a year. Police rush down the stairs, hop in their car and chase after the man. Red lights skipped, speed limit high and breaking all road laws. *Smash!* Kezzie crashes into the gate at Buckingham Palace, guards and police rush after the man...

Aidan Leamy (13)
Woodcote High School, Coulsdon

WHAT HAPPENED?

I crashed to the ground. A sudden wave of light swept over my eyes. Confused, angry and lightheaded, I realised that I had been hit. Where was I? Everything was a blur, and I knew that I had shattered the glass door to pieces, that I'd fallen into, cutting my skin and making it bleed. A pool of red surrounded me.

I pulled myself up, to try and remember what had happened. The view was distorted, and I was in a very precarious position. A metallic smell of vivid red blood permeated through the air and filled my lungs...

Eleanor Robson (14)
Woodcote High School, Coulsdon

GROOM SLAUGHTER

The sound of the siren was making my ears ring. The lights of the police cars were blinding me. I went over to the taped-up crime scene. A shattered wine bottle: one big shard the shade of olive-green was smothered in thick red blood. The shard was impaled in the groom's gut. With a lump in my throat, I told the hefty policeman next to me, "I need to see the suspect." He agreed and took me to the police van. Sitting nervously, the bride looked up at me and snarled. Her dress was covered in bright liquid red.

Jiya Vadher (13)
Woodcote High School, Coulsdon

THE SHADOW

Pitter-patter, pitter-patter. The footsteps travelled down the corridor. No person to be seen just a shadow and silence. This corridor was about 50 yards long, with just a door at the end of it. You walk down it with constant fear not knowing if you're going to be attacked.

Right foot, left foot. Step by step, getting closer and closer to the door. *Bang*. A loud crash from behind. The shadow keeps going and going. The shadow is grabbed, chucked around and dragged through the door. Loud screams followed.

Austen Barnhurst
Woodcote High School, Coulsdon

IT WAS BACK

She twisted the door handle and lightly pushed it agape. Her eyes widened as she stepped into the bathroom which stood with puddles of blood and her eyes fixated on the words on the white-tiled wall which read: 'Turn around'. The bloodied words dripped down the wall, as she shoved her shaking hands into her hoodie pockets. Biting her quivering lip, her eyes locked with the creature stood before her. Her heart dropped. Its eyes boring into her own. She twisted the door handle slamming it behind her.
It was back.

Rebecca Kendall
Woodcote High School, Coulsdon

PEOPLE WILL BELIEVE WHAT YOU MAKE THEM

The volume crackled on the security camera volume as we saw the man sink the knife into the pedestrian. The police had left without thanks, looking for the convict. I turned on the computer and unlinked it from the camera. Funny what you can make people see, what you can make them believe. They'll never find the convict. He doesn't even exist, just pixels on a screen - all I need anyway. I go into my kitchen and open my secret door, retrieving my knife, stained red with the dark, sticky blood of a human...

Sydney Holdsworth (11)
Woodcote High School, Coulsdon

GETAWAY!

The transport was in sight - the plan had begun. They leapt onto the vehicle from the rooftop and smashed the windscreen. They threw the driver out of the car and sped off. They had their hideout in sight but then the sound of sirens blasted in their ears. With the police behind them, they had to do a quick 360 turn. With some quick thinking, they detached the cargo and turned around. The cops were right in front of them. They sped up the car to full speed and jumped out. The cars collided with a huge explosion.

Toby Ward (12)
Woodcote High School, Coulsdon

CRIME OF PASSION

Lights of the police car were all I remembered. I was hiding the weapon. I remember his death. He was lying there motionless. I blanked out the sound, but I knew I'd heard screaming.

I woke up in the office. Police came in and asked me questions about that night. The night I struck him down. I couldn't remember anything. Just the lights, the blinding lights. They asked me why I killed him, the one I loved. I didn't know why but my hands were covered in blood. There was nothing I could do.

Lauren Curtis (12)
Woodcote High School, Coulsdon

FROM THE CRADLE TO THE GRAVE

I woke up to the ear-piercing sound of my child screaming and crying once again. When would this end? I grudgingly took the heavy duvet off my bed and pushed my feet into my slippers. It was pitch-black, so I had to cautiously feel my way downstairs and use my key to unlock the door. I grabbed the flashlight that was lying on the floor and turned it on. There she was. My baby. Still crying. She was still as pretty as ever. "Shh. Daddy's here." I said, kneeling next to her grave.

Abigail Hendle
Woodcote High School, Coulsdon

CAUGHT!

I walked away from the lifeless body, red dripping from my knife as the blood stalked behind me. I smirked. There was no way they could catch me. Dead of night, abandoned alleyway. It was all just too perfect!
My twin brother sat at the cafe; my alibi had been secured. My grin grew wider as a body had been reported to the police who were frantically searching for clues. I had left none. Next moment I had a gun in my face. "You're under arrest!" How had they found me?

Jamie Rouse (12)
Woodcote High School, Coulsdon

THE MYSTERIOUS SHADOW

The suspect was gone when I arrived at the crime scene. There was only blood on the floor and a broken window. In the corner of the room was a man who looked like he'd been shot a couple of times. I reached down to check his pulse... nothing. I needed to find the killer or else who knows what drama was going to go down. Then from behind the old door came a big black gloomy shadow. I held out my gun at the door but before I could see who it was, they were sprinting away...

Zachary Dallman (12)
Woodcote High School, Coulsdon

THE BODY

I arrived at the riverside. Rumours of a missing teenager from a holiday site had led me here. I pulled on my galoshes and jumped into the shallow, murky water, the sounds of police sirens ringing in my ears. Blue and red lights flashing in the corners of my eyes. Men in white overalls joined me in the river as we searched for the girl. Suddenly, one of the men yelled at me and I waded through the sludge to reach him. We hauled out the body, dread sinking into my stomach...

Veisa Zace
Woodcote High School, Coulsdon

A CRY FOR HELP

The week went by so slowly, it felt as if time stood still. Nothing felt right since Mike had died. I could feel this dark presence surrounding me, watching over my shoulder. I could deal with it until things started getting violent. I would wake up with marks on my legs and cups smashed outside my door. Maybe this wasn't Mike.

The haunting wasn't restricted to my home, things started to happen in public. I must've looked so stupid running away from nothing but to me, there was something there. A black figure. Was it here to take me?

Thea Clarkson (14)
XP East, Doncaster

I SAW RED

I wake from my slumber panicking, panting heavily. I struggle to recall the dream I've just experienced, but can only remember the emotions: alarm, terror, distress. I slowly stand on my quivering legs, and check my reflection - but I see nothing. I'm not reflected in the mirror! I put my hands to my head in alarm, and they come back a deep crimson, but I feel no pain. Spinning round, I see a still body on the bed I was just in, and a cluster of doctors looking grave and shaking their heads, crowding round the bed. I suddenly realise...

Ava Fletcher-Bedford (14)

XP East, Doncaster

THE GREY FIGURES!

There I was, looking down onto the surface of the strange planet. Something seemed odd. Something wasn't right. I was about to leave when I saw it. It just appeared out of nowhere. I received a hologram from the massive ship. The 2 tall, grey figures said something in an alien language. It was then that I heard the indistinguishable sound of something entering the hangar bay. I nervously checked the security cameras to find that they had been disabled. I heard a noise at the door and then I saw a white void. What had they done to me?

Lewis Floyd (13)
XP East, Doncaster

THE INSIDE JOB

Everybody was doing their own thing in the station, when screaming and shouting came from the hallway leading to the basement. Trails of blood led down the narrow hallway and down the stairs. All officers followed the tracks to find a body lying under a sheet. Parts of the building were shut off, only FBI and detectives had access. Most of the officers were in a room when Mark noticed that one person's badge had been tampered with and a few drops of blood were found on his chest. His heart began to race when he saw who it was...

Sami Fourie (13)
XP East, Doncaster

THE NOISE

I opened the door and entered the house, my torch lighting up the gloomy building. I signalled for my colleague to search the bottom floor while I went upstairs. I carefully tried to stay quiet as my boots creaked against the wooden floorboards. I reached upstairs and was met by a hallway with several doors. As I pondered which to start with a soft moan came from the door at the end of the hall. I crept across the pitch-black hall and opened the door shining my light on the source of the noise. What I saw shocked me forever.

Marcus Hague (14)

XP East, Doncaster

HIM

Eyes were blurry. Knees were weak. I'd taken more damage than I'd anticipated. At least the task was complete. I limped to a window in order to escape, only to turn back and see him staring back at me in the mirror. I resent the fact I resemble him, loathe even. I walked closer to the mirror. The glass shattered. I can't bear the fact to see him in me, although getting rid of the mirror calmed me almost, made me feel at ease. Today's events made us even. After all, he can no longer plague me. Goodbye, Dad.

Florence Roberts (14)
XP East, Doncaster

IT WILL ALL BE FINE!

I woke up to an emergency call from the police, explaining to me that my husband had been murdered on his way home from work. My throat tightened and my eyes filled with tears, causing my mascara to run violently down my cheeks. I couldn't sleep. I had to question where I went wrong. I had to question how they found him. I had to question if they found out the truth.

Later that day, I got called to visit the police station and be questioned. I memorised my story and remembered to stay calm. It will all be fine!

Ruby Underwood (13)

XP East, Doncaster

NEVER RING YOUR OWN NUMBER

One night, my friends and I had a sleepover. As a joke, we decided to call my number on my phone. We knew nothing would happen but it was worth a shot. Everyone continued to laugh and have fun, having pizza and watching movies. All getting sleepier we decided to go to sleep.

In the middle of the night, I got up to get a drink. Being all alone in the kitchen, I felt like someone was watching me, I brushed it off. Suddenly someone or something was at the window. I quickly woke the girls. Tensions were running high...

Lucie-Mae Cordell (13)
XP East, Doncaster

NOBODY THERE

I don't know what voice it was, or what opened the door. All I know is that it wasn't me. Never before had I seen such decay or felt like I was being watched so much before; I looked behind me, but there was nobody there. It wasn't my flashlight in the other room, nor was it my blood; I walked forward to take a closer look, but there was nobody there. Suddenly, I heard a piano playing, I walked forward to take a closer look, but there was nobody there. Suddenly I heard a loud laugh. Somebody was there!

Zak M-Hall (14)
XP East, Doncaster

RETURN

I wake up, and pull the covers off me and step onto the hardwood floor. I walk to the kitchen and get a bowl of Weetos and get into my Peel Trident and drive to work. As I arrive in my box studio I get called by my boss that I need to do some work on the field so I step up and walk into the urine-stained toilet stalls and get ready to go out to the location. As I get out of my car and the atmosphere changes I see the corpse, it's mine!
Bang!
I wake up.

Dylan Ap Harri (13)
XP East, Doncaster

YoungWriters®
— Est. 1991 —

YOUNG WRITERS
INFORMATION

We hope you have enjoyed reading this book – and that you will continue to in the coming years.

If you're a young writer who enjoys reading and creative writing, or the parent of an enthusiastic poet or story writer, visit our website **www.youngwriters.co.uk/subscribe** to join the World of Young Writers and receive news, competitions, writing challenges, tips, articles and giveaways! There is lots to keep budding writers motivated to write!

If you would like to order further copies of this book, or any of our other titles, then please give us a call or order via your online account.

Young Writers
Remus House
Coltsfoot Drive
Peterborough
PE2 9BF
(01733) 890066
info@youngwriters.co.uk

Join in the conversation!
Tips, news, giveaways and much more!

 YoungWritersUK   @YoungWritersCW   YoungWritersCW